♥

Always Right Here

ALWAYS RIGHT HERE

JENNIFER WALTERS

UNTITLED

CHAPTER 1

JANUARY 2017

I opened my eyes and the white walls stared back at me, glowing from the light shining in from the hallway. So much noise, phones ringing, people talking. It was hard to focus on the picture on the wall without my glasses on. Where are my glasses? I wanted them, needed them to see.

I eased my head to the left and saw the remote, just inches from my hand. I picked up my fingers with the weight of them resting on my palm and wrist. I closed my eyes and focused on lifting them together. I felt them shake, opened my eyes to acknowledge my progress. My pointer finger drifted as my hand jerked to the left. One button, just one button. I felt the remote cold beneath my hand. Pressure. I just needed to find it. I moved my hand around, unable to see it. I felt a circular bubble beneath my middle finger. I pushed hard three times, not knowing whether it would send for help.

I heard a noise coming from behind me and knew he was there. I could feel his breath in my hair. He inched his way closer, planting a kiss on my forehead, startling me.

"What do you need, honey?"

My peripheral vision was disappointing me, along with the blurriness in my right eye. I relaxed as he stared into my eyes and ran his fingers through my long brown curls. His touch was gentle, letting go before his hands got stuck in the snarls of my matted, unwashed hair. The consequence of being in a bed for two days, maybe three, I couldn't be sure.

I opened my mouth to talk, but my tongue felt thick and dry, I could not get any words out.

"Shush," he whispered, smiling at me and ran the back of his hand over my left cheek. I felt goosebumps run down my arm, but I fought to keep my heavy eyes open. I tried to move my right arm, grab for the Rosary next to the small stuffed bear that propped up my arm. The more I fought to take control, the more tired I became. It took all the strength I had just to keep my eyes open.

He walked down to the end of the bed and uncovered my feet. He grabbed them both and began rubbing them just the way he knew I liked it. I closed my eyes, feeling a little dizzy and shaky, but I tried to focus on feeling his touch on my right foot.

His massage was gentle and slow, but I was nauseous. I could not enjoy it at all, no matter how hard I tried. Tears restricted my view and left me feeling sorry for myself. This was the only way I could show any emotion. I focused on the path my tear took as it made its way down my cheek and stopped right beneath my chin.

His reaction of complete cessation of movement startled me as he promptly made his way to my side and lightly wiped away any evidence of my tears. I knew he was struggling with my absence of emotions, and this tear brought him hope. I could tell he was scared and wasn't sure what to do.

He reached across the table behind him and grabbed my glasses. The queen of diamonds playing card taped to the lens and made me giggle to myself that he always figured out a way to solve a problem, no matter how strange. The card helped my eye to focus since I lost most of the vision in the other eye, and when uncovered, it made me dizzy.

I was glad I told them this before I could no longer talk. I wasn't sure when I was hallucinating or when he was really there. Sometimes my dreams felt so real, and sometimes what I thought was real was actually a dream. I was sure it was the painkillers they had me on.

At first I was sure I had a stroke, but the doctors assured me it was just a side effect of the brain tumor.

"How are you feeling today, honey? Squeeze my hand once for good, twice for not so good." He stared into my eyes and watched me focus on my hand. I squeezed his hand once with everything I had, which left me exhausted. He smiled because he knew how hard I tried.

"Have I told you how beautiful you look today?" He rubbed my hand softly as he sat on the side of my bed. I could only imagine this hot mess that lay before him, although I believed he meant what he said by the love in his eyes.

I tried to smile and wondered if he could tell. Every time I blinked, I had to force my eyes to open again. I wanted more than anything to stay in this moment with him. Another tear released, and I felt it trapped beneath the rim of my glasses. It tickled, and I was frozen, unable to wipe the irritability away.

He wiped away the trace of my unhappiness with a single swipe of his thumb, as if he had heard my silent vociferation.

He grabbed something else off the table. The sponge came toward me and I opened my mouth in desperation. I tried to guide the water down my throat without the help of my tongue. The damp sponge felt so good as the water ran down my throat, making me cough. My brain no longer was in control of my body. He placed the sponge back into the water and wet my mouth a few more times until I had had enough and pursed my lips in response. How could it be so much work just to swallow?

I saw a shadow entering the room and watched the nurse as she found her way to the computer hanging on the wall. The frigid open room sent a chill throughout my body, nipping at my soul.

"Good morning, Destiny," she said with a smile, too big to be real. Who was she to come in so happy when I could not even move? She was probably going home to her doctor husband and they would probably kiss and go on about their day without her even realizing how lucky she was to talk to him, to kiss him.

I coughed, choking on the giant muscle I once used to converse. I tried and failed to move it, wanting to return the small greeting, but I no longer had that luxury of communication.

"How are you feeling?" she asked, like I could really answer her.

She seemed to ignore my husband, and I wondered if he was annoying her with his jokes. Sometimes he thought he was a lot funnier than he really was. He didn't understand when he was pushing the jokes just a little too far and he always needed me when to tell him to quit.

I felt my body temperature suddenly rising and my face getting warm. What did I do to deserve being trapped in my body? Was God punishing me for something? Would I ever be able to talk again? Why me? What did I do to deserve this?

I wanted to scream, feel the satisfaction of breaking something with my own two hands. I desired the feel of my husband's hands on my body again, the sexual desire we once had. I silently scolded myself as my eyes once again filled with tears, which made me feel vulnerable and downhearted.

The beautiful blonde nurse reminded me of a nurse I once knew, long ago. A woman who came in between my husband and me. I did not care to think about it, not right now. She gently lifted the arm I could not feel and began taking my vitals.

"It's a great day to be inside, Destiny. It's close to fifty below out there, brr." She smiled at me, knowing I wouldn't, couldn't respond. I saw my husband folding up the sheet in the chair that had become his abode. He put the flannel shirt I bought him long ago for Christmas over his t-shirt. He moved to replace where the nurse had stood. He leaned over the hospital bed, kissing my dry, cracked lips. Although I couldn't kiss him back, I relaxed my lips and closed my eyes, feeling his soft lips against mine. I didn't want him to pull away, didn't want him to stop. I felt the electric current pass through our bodies, leaving me feeling grounded, an escape from the reality of being terminal.

"The nurse will take good care of you. I will go get some coffee in the lounge and I will be right back," he said. He smiled at me with his beautiful prominent dimples, halfway hidden beneath his scruffy whiskers. "I love you," he said, resting his forehead against mine. He pulled away and wiped his eyes.

I wanted to tell him I loved him back. I wanted to scream it, jump out of the bed and wrap my arms around him and never let go. My heart felt like it would beat right out of my chest. I struggled to take control of my body with no success. It only left me feeling fatigued and deflated.

I had no dignity left. I couldn't run, cook dinner, wash

myself, or even drink a glass of water on my own. I couldn't even tell my husband I loved him. I closed my eyes as he faded off into the distance. I wished for an answer to my prayers to talk again, just once before I died.

The nurse changed into my hospital gown. Although I've always been quite conservative, my body exposed seemed small compared to the things that really mattered to me now. I was a fifty-one-year-old woman on hospice. After the surgery tomorrow, I wondered if I would still be alive to have the chance to talk again.

The nurse turned me on my side, leaving a gateway for my tears to escape with gravity. She fluffed my pillows, lifted my head gently and then lay the pillows back beneath my head. I was a prisoner in my body. I blinked away the pain and gave up trying to stay awake, for I knew my only solace was in my dreams.

CHAPTER 2

JANUARY 1991

J woke up naked and cold, my red satin sheets covering everything but my toes. I could smell the rancid Kahlua seeping out of my pores and the sour taste of Colorado Bulldogs lingering on my breath. I rolled over to grab the other pillow to cover my atrocious headache.

"Ouch!" a male voice yelled. My arm stopped mid-air by his face. My eyes shot open, and I held my breath, my pulse throbbing in my stomach and chest. We both sat up quickly. I got lost in his beautiful blue eyes for only a second as I focused on making sure they completely covered my naked breasts. He held his hand over his eye in pain, laughing.

I shot him my best death glare and let out an annoyed sigh.

The sun blared through the East window, burning my eyes and intensifying my headache. It was quite deceiving considering it was mid-January in northern Minnesota.

He saluted me, teasing me with his sexy dimples, and smiled. Ugh, he took nothing seriously. I pulled the blankets from him with a hard yank and he sat there naked.

"Don't worry, I'm okay. Sure, you can have the blanket," he said, ignoring me not apologizing.

I couldn't help but stare at his defined biceps and six-pack.

I looked down a little further and noticed he was at full attention and not even trying to cover himself up with the down comforter rolled up at the bottom of his feet, within reach. He had a grin on his face. I turned away quickly, pretending I didn't see a thing.

I silently scolded myself for the shots of Patron and Colorado Bulldogs and that moment of weakness that led me to bed with him. I shook my head and closed my eyes for a moment, trying to figure out how I got here.

"Where are my clothes!" It was more of a demand than a question.

I heard the bed creak as he made his way behind me. What was he doing? I felt something land on my face. I opened up my mouth, ready to yell at him for throwing stuff at me, then I saw the red lace and snatched it from his hand. I slipped my arms through my bra and pulled the cups over the satin sheet covering me.

"How the hell did this happen?"

"You don't remember?"

I focused on last night. Drinks at the bar, a couple shots, coming back to the house with him...oh no. I vividly remember dancing in my living room.

"I don't how you could forget," he said, shaking his finger at me. "We came home, you told me you wanted to show me what I was missing—"

"That's enough!" I said, wanting him to stop talking. I felt my face burning hot.

I now remembered dancing while he sat on the couch, ripping off my clothes and throwing them at him.

"Let's just say you put Shannon Tweed to shame," he laughed.

I could hear him putting on his clothes as he rambled on. I struggled to clasp my bra around the sheet.

"Need any help with that?"

"No!" I snapped, holding the sheet securely in my teeth, still struggling to fasten my bra. My arms became tired as I tried to pull harder to gain slack so I could clasp it and get the hell out of here. I just about had it closed when the sheet pulled out of my mouth and fell to the floor before I could grab it. "Damn it!"

I bent down quickly to pull the sheet back up and turned to see if he was looking. Of course he was.

"Quite a view." He grinned. "You know, if you would have just let me help you, you wouldn't be struggling so much." He walked behind me, softly taking the place of my hands and clasping it.

I quickly adjusted the cups in place.

"Thank you," I said, turning around to face him.

He was standing there in his boxer briefs. I couldn't help but stare at the defined lines running down the inside of his hip bones as they rode a little too low on his waist. He was doing this just to make a mockery of me.

I turned around and spotted something red in the hall-way. I ran toward it, holding the sheet as I bent down to pick up my underwear.

I peeked down the hall and saw my clothes hanging over the side of the couch, just where they should have been. The thought of me seducing him with my notorious lap dance made even sicker to my stomach. I remembered him throwing me over his shoulder as he slapped my butt, heading to the bedroom.

I need to get out of here, fast. Months without sex and a moment of weakness; I blame the alcohol. I heard his zipper as he stepped into the hallway, coming closer to me as I finished putting on my shirt with my back to him. I pushed the picture of him shirtless and defined out of my head and turned around.

"Sorry if you got the wrong impression. I still want a divorce and I will come back to get my stuff when you are at work," I said. His face instantly desiccated. I grabbed my stilettos off the floor and carried them in my hand, slamming the door behind me.

6 WEEKS LATER

THE RINGING OF MY PARENTS' hallway phone woke me from a deep sleep.

I rolled my eyes when the ringing would not stop and knew it was probably my mom calling. If I chose not to answer, she would come home from work and pull me out of bed again.

"Hello," I said in my perkiest voice.

"Please tell me you aren't still sleeping, Destiny. It's nearly two in the afternoon."

"Mom, I'm not sleeping. I was actually just getting out of the shower," I said. I stood up and found myself more clean pajamas.

"I'm sorry, I'm just worried about you, honey. You lay in bed most of the day and are up most of the night. You really need to find a job. You need to talk to your husband, he misses you. Are you taking the pills the doctor gave you?"

"Mom, please, stop,"I said, rolling my eyes and heading to

the bathroom down the hall. "I am an adult, you know." I put my nose to my armpit and made a sour face at the strong stench.

"Destiny, you can't live your life like this. You are twenty-four years old. Act like it. Someone needs to put some sense into you. Bryan has been stopping over two to three times a week to see you and you lock yourself in the bedroom. Last week he only came once. You will lose him, you know that?" Her tone brought me back to my teenage years, a time I didn't want to think about.

"Mom, this is my life. If I am imposing, fine I'll move out, but just stay out of my life!" I screamed.

"Destiny Marie. He's your husband. You haven't even been married a year. You need to talk to him. This isn't the way marriage works."

"Like you're one to talk. I got to go, Mom." I hung up the phone and unplugged it from the wall.

I undressed and felt the water in the shower with the back of my hand before stepping in. The warm shower felt good as it ran down my body. I turned around and let it hit me in the face, placing my hands on the wall. A sudden dizzy spell took me by surprise, leaving me struggling to keep my balance. I was having a hard time catching my breath. The room was spinning, and I felt as though I would pass out. Bowing my head and gripping the wall tighter helped me feel a little steadier. I turned the water to cold, but it didn't seem to help. I switched off the shower, realizing there was no way I could wash my hair feeling this dizzy and weak.

I wrapped the towel around me and didn't even try to dry off. The wallpaper in the hallway looked like a Victoria's Secret bag, I noticed while making my way down the hall to my old bedroom. It was now a half junk room, half guest bedroom with a tiny table in the corner. I shut the door and crawled under my sheets, towel still wrapped around me. Struggling to take a full breath, I felt sick to my stomach, the room spinning. I wondered if maybe low blood sugar could cause this or even a side effect of the Prozac I was on.

I laid in bed, wide awake in the fetal position for about an hour before starting to feel better. It was time to eat something. I was still feeling a little light-headed when I sat up. Taking my time wrapping my towel a little tighter under my arms, I slowly stood up. I put on my bathrobe and held onto the railing as I walked downstairs into the kitchen. The cupboards were slightly bare, not much food to choose from.

I found a small Hershey's bar and took a few bites as I made my way back upstairs, much slower than normal. I took out my abnormal psychology book and placed it on the small table in my room. I bent down to grab my highlighter and felt the sudden pain in my stomach rise.

I made a run in the bathroom's direction. As I headed down the hall, I could feel the acid burning along my esophagus. I gave up my candy bar and heaved out anything else that was in my stomach. I stayed there a few moments on my knees and cried until I had the energy to get up and brush my teeth. I got dressed and crawled onto the couch to watch the daytime soaps.

"Are you finally up and moving?" Mom said, walking in the door. "I see you moved from lying in your bed to lying on the couch." I rolled my eyes.

"Are you okay? You don't look good. You look pale. Are you pregnant?"

"No, Mom, get off my case," I said, deciding to go upstairs.I walked past her and had to sit on the recliner, feeling too dizzy to continue walking.

"Destiny, take a test just to ease your mind," she said with a pat on my shoulder. After a few moments of me not saying anything, she added, a little more sternly, "Destiny, promise me you will take a pregnancy test if this continues. You haven't been throwing up, have you?"

"No, Mom," I said. "It's just a bug."

CHAPTER 3

J found myself at Jill's house, plastic Kmart bag dangling from my fingers behind my back. I rang the doorbell and opened the door.

"Jill," I called out as I walked in, taking off my shoes and closing the door.

"I'm in here," she said. "I'm just making dinner."

"Okay, I'll be there in a second, I have to use your bathroom," I said. I ran straight into the bathroom without being seen. I turned around once safely inside, standing with my back against the door. I pulled the box out of the bag and opened it quietly, taking a deep breath and letting out a sigh.

After I finished, I brought the stick out with me and headed into the kitchen.

No trace of any lines on the two windows on the test yet. Jill was cutting up tomatoes. My sister and I were very close growing up. My mom left my dad in the middle of the night with us to get away from the abuse. I will never forget the screams that came from their bedroom that night. Sure there had been a quite a few incidents, but this time her eye was black, her lip cracked open, she had a cracked lip—she did not find out until weeks later when she was having a hard time breathing—but the worst part was he threatened to kill my sister and me. Mom said she had it. It was as though as long as he was only hitting her, it was okay or something. She did not understand that was traumatic for us to see. My sister was a baby, but I was old enough to remember. My mother was brave, much braver than I was. She had her own struggles with mental health, and I knew that was probably the reason I had a hard time staying awake during the day and sleeping at night. I hated that I was depressed, but the stress with Bryan was killing me.

"Hey, Dez," she said, looking up to greet me. "What's that?" She pointed to the stick in my hand.

"It's a pregnancy test. I'm sure I'm not pregnant, but I'm just taking a test to prove mom wrong."

She laughed, "You need to stop letting her get to you."

I put the test down on the counter. "I know, but I just wasn't feeling well this morning. Mom is driving me crazy," I said, rolling my eyes and putting a cube of tomato in my mouth.

"That's for my salad, Dez. If you want one, all you have to do is ask."

I glanced down at the pregnancy test; my eyes widened with fear. "Two blue lines. What does that mean?" I ran to the bathroom to take the box out of the garbage and brought it back to the kitchen.

"What does it say?" she said, looking over my shoulder at the box.

"Two blue lines, two blue lines. Here it is," I said, pointing to the instructions. "Oh, no!" I exclaimed, dropping the box and covering my mouth and nose with my hands.

"Dez!" she said, bending down to pick it up. She wiped her wet hands on her jeans. "You can't be," she said, almost as panicked as I was as she also read the words."How? Who?"

"Seriously? You are asking me who? I'm married, Jill, I'm not a slut. We aren't divorced yet."

"Oh, I know that," she said, putting a hand on my shoulder. "But when did you guys—"

"Six weeks ago, when I tried to talk to him about getting a divorce. A few shots of tequila and Colorado Bulldogs turned into a striptease and a morning full of regrets. Ugh, what am I going to do?" I said, my eyes watering. I crossed my arms and bowed my head. Ashamed for being so irresponsible.

Jill put her arms around me, and our heads knocked together.

I leaned in and put my head on her shoulder, refusing to uncross my arms.

I pulled away. "What am I going to do, Jill. What am I going to tell him?"

"Slow down, Dez, it will be okay. Bryan will be stoked. He would do anything to have you back in his life. Can you imagine how amazing he would be as a father? That baby would have the best dad in the world."

"What, you don't think I'd make a wonderful mother?"

"Of course I do, Dez."

I glared at her.

"I was just saying he would be supportive."

"I guess."

"Now, mom—"

"Ugh, Mom. Why does she have to be right? I'm sorry, Jill, I didn't mean to snap at you. I'm just so sick of everyone telling me how perfect Bryan is and how good Bryan is, I'm just sick of being married to a man who everyone thinks is sooo perfect. I know I have to try to save my marriage, but sometimes I just want to break away from Mr. Perfect because I'm not perfect myself. I love him, I'm just sick of feeling like a nobody and always being referred to as Bryan's wife. You do not understand what it is like. Ugh, it's hard to describe. I mean, I'm so in love with him, I just never feel good enough."

"Destiny, you understand how dumb that sounds, right? I mean, poor you, married to an amazing man everyone loves who treats you like a princess. Don't shut him out, you need to go over there right now and tell him. He needs to know before he finds out some other way."

"I get that, Jill. I understand how dumb it sounds coming out of my mouth, but I can't help the way I feel. I will go over there and tell him. I did something terrible and I just feel so guilty, it's eating at me."

"You need to move on from whatever you did and start fresh with him."

"I just don't think I can forgive myself for what I did."

"Do you love him?"

"I love him." Bryan was my person, and I hated not being able to be around him. If he knew what I did, he would never speak to me again, anyway. Now I was pregnant with his child. How was I going to run away now?

"Keep an open mind and give it some time. Take my advice and don't tell him whatever it is that's been eating at you. I don't even want to know what it is, you need to move on, we all make mistakes. Don't let him get away, Dez. Any woman would die to have a man like him."

"That's the problem."

Jill placed her hands on my shoulder and spun me around to face her.

"Promise me you will at least give him a chance, for the baby and for you."

I nodded, gave her a big hug and opened the door to let myself out.

"Thanks, Jill, for having no filter. I needed that."

"That's what sisters are for. Now call me right after you

talk to him, I'm dying here! Oh, and Destiny, you will be a great mom," she said, continuing to cut up her veggies.

PULLING UP TO HIS HOUSE, I shifted my car into park and stared at our house. I thought about a tiny child running around outside our home. Would he ever forgive me if he found out what I did? At this point all I could do was to continue on with my life as though it never happened and hope he did not find out. I could see him in the window, vacuuming the living room. I made my way to the house and stared at him for just a moment, watching the way his head tilted and his muscles bulged beneath his tight blue shirt. I remembered how he took such pride in everything he did, and I smiled. I walked up the stairs and wondered if I should knock at my own house or just go right in. I opened the storm door and knocked loudly. His face lit up as he opened the door, seeing it was me.

"Dez," he said. He pulled me into a big hug. He took a step back and put both of his hands in his jean pockets as if he was afraid of my reaction. "Come in. You don't have to knock, this is your house too."

I leaned in and surprised myself as I kissed him on the lips, much longer than I should have. I had been wanting to do that for so long. Surprised, he kissed me back gently and pulled me in as if this was the last kiss we would ever share. Maybe he thought I was here to say goodbye or file for divorce. I pulled my head back with my arms over his shoulders and grasped behind his neck. I stared into his eyes, trying to find the words for what I needed to say. I ran my fingers through his hair and he stared back in disbelief.

"Hello, Bryan."

He shot me a curious smile.

"I've missed you," I said in a whisper.

"You have no idea. Does this mean you are coming home now?"

"Well, I have something to tell you."

He looked concerned, and we both dropped our arms. I stood there silent as I tried to find the words.

"Is everything okay?" he finally said.

"Um, Bryan, I just want you to know I am so sorry for everything I have put you through. I have been trying to find myself and in the process I have taken you down with me. Today I was sick, and I thought it was the depression, but I took a test just be sure and well, I'm pregnant."

His mouth hung open, and he just stared at me.

"I know this is a lot to take in. I'm going to keep the baby, Bryan, and if you want be a part of our life, I'm ready to make this work. But if you aren't—"

"No," he put his arms around me. "I just didn't expect that. I needed to process what you were saying for a second. I want this too, Dez. You know I want nothing more than to be with you."

"You would give us another shot?" I said. I was so horrible to him. I had been ignoring his phone calls for weeks and not giving him an explanation at all, and he was still willing to give us another shot.

"My life couldn't be more complete than it is right now. The real question is, when are you moving back in?" He picked me up, and I wrapped my legs around him. He spun me in a circle, slowly letting me down so he could kiss me, and then bent down in front of me to lift my shirt and kiss my belly.

"Hello little boy or girl," he said. "I do not know how to be a dad, but I promise I will do the best I can. I know you are just a teeny tiny pea but you have the best mommy in the whole world and we will be one big happy family, I promise."

He stood up and kissed me again. "When should I go get your stuff from your mom's house?"

"I have to go to school, so I won't really be around to help today."

"That's okay, I can go to your mom's and get your stuff," he said.

"Then maybe I will stay here tonight after I'm done with school?"

His dimples showed. "I would absolutely love that. I have to work later, but I will have a surprise waiting for you when you come home. Destiny, welcome home," he said. "Please never leave again. This is right where we belong, together."

CHAPTER 4

"*I*t's seven o'clock, Dez. Why didn't you call me after you talked to Bryan? I've been dying here," she said. "How did it go?"

Jill was a single mom and loved living vicariously through me. She did not want a man in her life and decided she was no longer looking. She was off the market. She was busy with her daughter and taking care of a mom who was the perfect example of an addict. Growing up, she used alcohol to numb her fear of dad finding her. Jill told her if dad would find her, he would have by now.

"I'm sorry Jill, I was running late for school and I just didn't get a chance to call."

"And..." She said, tapping her foot.

"Well, I got there, and he was vacuuming so I debated whether I should knock."

"You didn't, did you? It is your house, and it's not like Bryan would care."

I nodded. "Well he saw me, but it was weird not knowing where I stood. So anyway, I told him about the baby, it just came out and he was in shock at first but thrilled." I spun my wedding ring around my finger.

"I take it you are back together. You are staring at your ring like you just saw it for the first time."

"You know me well," I said.

"Well, where is he and why are you here at my house and not with him?"

I sat down on her couch. "He said he would work tonight, but he would move my stuff from mom's house while I was at school today. He said he had a surprise for me."

"A surprise? I bet mom was ecstatic that he was moving you out of there. Does she know you are pregnant yet?"

I hit her in the shoulder. "Hey! I'm sure mom loves having me around."

"Sure she does," she said, a smirk spreading across her face.

I shrugged. "But God no, I'm not telling her I'm pregnant until I have to. I am staying at home tonight and I was hoping you would drive over there with me," I said. "I am a little nervous moving in may be a little too much too soon since we've been split up for weeks, you know? To be honest, it just doesn't feel like my home there anymore. I think that's why he would have a surprise waiting for me. He knows me."

"The reason you have been on a break was because of something you think you did that he won't forgive you. It's all in your head but I'm your sister so of course I will go over there with you. What do you think the surprise is?" Jill put on her jacket and boots.

"I don't know, to be honest. I was thinking about what he would have gotten me the entire drive home from school. I figured it had to have something to do with the baby, but that was as far as I could guess."

"I'm sure you're right.

"Let's stop and get something to eat on the way," I said.

"You are just worried he might still be there when you get there."

I got into her car. "You're probably right."

WHEN WE FINALLY GOT TO my house and opened up the door, it looked like a baby shower. There were pink and blue confetti trains leading up the stairs and balloons and streamers to match, hanging from the ceiling. Jill and I looked at each other and did what any curious girl would do, we followed it. We raced to see who could get to the end of it first and I won, although I'm sure she let me. It leads us right into the guest bedroom. Opening the door, I was surprised to find samples of baby paint colors taped to the wall, three beautiful baby pink dresses and two blue sleepers, *What to Expect When You're Expecting*, a three hundred dollar gift card to Baby Gap, and another gift card for Kmart laid out on the floor like it was Christmas. He knew how much I loved going shopping.

"Holy crap, Dez! He went all out."

I turned around to see what she was looking at and spotted two boxes of newborn diapers and a big package of baby wipes. There was baby lotion, shampoo, and diaper rash cream, along with an ear thermometer and a note with Bryan's handwriting taped to the package with a big pink bow. I opened it, revealing a beautiful jogging stroller.

Jill raised her eyebrows at the gift. She knew how much I loved to run. She then held the note in her hand and read it aloud.

"Dear Dez," she said, grinning at me. "I could not be more ecstatic than when you showed up at the front door of our home and revealed we were having a baby. Don't get me wrong, I was shocked, but I know together we will be the best parents any child could ever ask for. To think of this tiny little human inside you is half you and half me, I can only imagine how beautiful and loving he or she will be. I know you would love to pick out the crib and all the other baby accessories, but I had to get just a few things to show how excited I am. Since the day we met, I have fallen more and more in love with you, and although there have been some hard times, I can only think of this as a fresh start and a new beginning for our everlasting marriage." She stopped reading and looked at me while I just fingered the box containing the running stroller.

"I want you to know that if you want to take this relation-ship slowly, I understand completely and I won't rush anything until you are ready. I will always wait with open arms when you are ready for me to share the bedroom with you. For now, I think it is important you get the king-size bed in our room for you and our tiny little fetus, where you will be the most comfortable. I love you more than the world and I can't wait until the day I can go to sleep and wake up every morning—that I don't have to work midnights—with you by my side. I have heard pregnant women get strange cravings and I just want you to know no matter what time of day, I am only a phone call away and I will run to the store if you want pickles and peanut butter or whatever pregnant people crave. I love you both with all my heart and soul. Love, Bryan."

"Wow," I said, the only word I could think to describe this extreme gesture. It did not surprise me at all because that was who Bryan was.

"Wow, is right. He really loves you, I'm so jealous. Let's go check out the bedroom," Jill said, running out the door and leaving me alone.

I followed her into my bedroom where the bed was made to perfection and a body pillow laid on top. I sat down and touched the three foot long feathered pillow. It was the best gift he could have possibly given me.

"I cannot believe he bought you a body pillow. How can you not be head over heels for him?" She picked it up and squished it, rubbing the soft cotton fabric across my face. "How did you ever let this guy go?"

I realized he must have spent the entire day getting the house ready for my arrival, including getting all my stuff from my mom's and putting it all away. I assumed he sent his mom, Judy, shopping to help get all this stuff for the baby. Everything was back where it was when I was living there many weeks ago.

Jill opened up my closet. "Seriously? He color coordinated your clothes, Dez."

I ran over to the closet. "I can't believe he did that. And I can't believe he bought me a jogging stroller."

"You two love your running, don't you? That was so thoughtful. Aren't you excited?"

"I am. I just feel a little anxious, that's all. It's a lot."

"How can you feel anxious? I mean, look at all the thought he put into this homecoming. Look at this pillow, for god's sake, it's almost as long as me. He did this all in one day? I can't believe it.

I shrugged. My secret digging deep inside my heart. "It's been a long day. I'm exhausted."

She put her hand on my shoulder. "Why don't you lay down and go to bed. Oh, and Dez, maybe you should ask him if he wants to go shopping with you to pick out more stuff for the baby. It is the least you can do after he did all of this. Don't be stubborn, sis," she said.

"We'll see. How are you going to get home?"

"I'm going to walk to Michael's, maybe go out for a little bit. He's only a couple blocks from here."

"Ok, Jill. Be safe and thank you," I said. As soon as she left, I wrapped my body around the pillow and hugged it tight. This would be the best night of sleep I'd had in weeks. I was finally home.

THE SMELL of bacon lured me out of bed around noon. I slipped my robe on that was hanging on the back of the closet door, right where it used to be. I tiptoed down the stairs and saw Bryan humming while cooking an omelet and taking bacon out of the skillet. He looked so focused, so happy, so at ease. I could not help but smile in admiration. He turned around, heading toward the kitchen table, smiling when he saw me.

"Careful, hot pan coming through. Good morning, beautiful." He greeted me as though nothing had changed, with a kiss on my forehead and with no hesitation or awkwardness. He walked past me to the table where he finished filling the plates full of breakfast. "How did you sleep?"

"Very well, thanks to that body pillow. It felt so good to be back in my—our bed." I corrected myself, hoping he hadn't noticed. "Thank you, Bryan. For everything."

"It was no problem. I am glad you liked it. Maybe you want to take a break from your homework today and go shopping. I have four days off, so if you need anything, I'll be around." He sat down in the chair across from me and took a bite of his omelet.

I couldn't seem to muster the energy to eat. "That was really a great surprise to come home to. You really didn't have to do that. I want you to know how much I appreciate it." I moved my eggs around a little on my plate. "I was wondering if maybe you wanted to take a drive to Duluth and we could pick out a crib and changing table together. If you aren't too tired that is. If not I don't mind going, I just thought that maybe you would want to come." I stared at my plate and wondered why I was rambling.

He got up, walked around to my chair and kneeled down, placing his pointer finger and thumb on my chin as he gently tilted my face to meet his.

"Destiny, there is nothing I would rather do then spend the day shopping with you." He gently kissed my forehead and stared at me for a moment before walking to the fridge to pour us both a glass of orange juice.

"Oh, not for me, thank you," I said. "I've been a little sick to my stomach. And with how acidic orange juice is, I just don't think it would be a very good idea. To tell you the truth, this looks so good, but I may have to start with just a few saltines before I eat something solid."

"No problem, I didn't even know you had morning sickness. I'm so sorry, I didn't know. He grabbed my plate and covered it with plastic wrap.

"You are doing everything I could imagine, thank you. Don't be sorry at all. I will get changed so we can get shopping. Ten minutes sound good?" I grabbed a glass of water and he handed me a package of saltines while I made my way up the stairs to get ready.

"Sounds good."

THE HOUR-AND-A-HALF DRIVE was the opposite of silent, like I had expected it to be. I hated having to go so far just to shop, because Hibbing was so small. Although we have a Kmart, our mall didn't have many stores. Duluth was an hour and fifteen minute drive from Hibbing.

Bryan talked about his job and how much he loved it. He told me he liked to put his police car in the garage so he didn't scare off the neighbors. He talked about the sheriffs he worked with and how great they all got along. He told me it hasn't been the same without me around and admitted to sleeping on my side of the bed every night. He said that was the only way he could fall to sleep.

From there it turned a little less serious and I told him about school and that I would take a little time off after this semester to focus on my pregnancy and taking care of our baby full-time. He was very supportive, as I expected him to be. "We will make it work," he said. "Let me worry about the finances so you can just focus on being healthy."

He was great shopping with me all day and carried all of our purchases. I could tell he was getting exhausted from staying up all night. We bought a white crib and matching diaper changing table and dresser for the baby's room. They couldn't deliver it for two weeks, but we agreed there was no rush. We bought a few outfits, bibs, and onesies. I made him stop at Barnes and Noble, and I looked around while he searched for a new Tom Clancy book. After, we had lunch at Olive Garden.

"I have a surprise, Bryan." I said, pulling a book out of the Barnes and Noble bag.

"*Guide to Running While Pregnant*," he read aloud. "So, I take it you want to use that running stroller, then?" I handed him the book, and he turned it over to look at the back with a big grin on his face.

"Are you kidding, it is the best present in the world. Thank you. You really didn't have to do that, but I'm so glad you did. I've heard a lot of talk about running while pregnant and how it makes for an easier labor as long as it isn't over-strenuous and thought maybe we could run together again."

"I thought you'd never ask," he said. He put his hand on mine across the table. "I will never forget the day I bumped into you in college when we were both running."

I laughed. "Me neither. How can I forget you running right into me?"

"Oh, no, you ran right into me," he said.

I got butterflies just thinking about that day. "Okay, well, I had to. How else would you have noticed me?"

"Wait, did you do that on purpose?" he said. He leaned back in his chair and crossed his arms with a smirk on his face.

"I told you I had the hots for you in high school, Mr. Prom King. I never thought I had a chance, and then a few years later I moved all the way to Bemidji to go to college and there you were. I expected to see Olivia close by, but she wasn't, so I knew I needed to make a move while I had the chance." I giggled at the memory.

"You never told me that before. I may not have known who you were in high school, Dez, but I saw you that day running in those little black shorts and I may have pretended not to see you. So you didn't know she moved away that day when you saw me?"

"No, not at the time. I thought you two would end up together forever, I think everyone did," I said. I leaned in closer. "Wait a minute, so you ran into me? All this time I thought I made the move, but we had the same intentions?"

"Yes, I couldn't help myself, look at you."

"Oh stop," I said as I batted my eyelashes. "You were a big hockey player, so I guess the thought of you being attracted to me at the time seemed near impossible." I fingered my wedding ring in my lap.

"Not to mention, you were the most beautiful girl in the school, even if you were only a freshman," he said, winking and smiling at me. His perfect teeth and sexy dimples made me feel like that young girl the day we ran into each other.

"Remember the bridge?" He asked.

"How could I forget? It was so romantic. We'd ditch class

and meet on the hidden bridge in the middle of the woods. It was really romantic. Those were the days," I said.

"Sometimes we would just chat for hours on that bridge. It was a great running trail too."

"Oh, I remember," I said. "Sometimes when I would get stressed I'd go sit on the bridge and listen to mother nature. It was great meditation for the soul."

He stared at me in a way that made me feel guilty. It was passionate, like he was lucky to have me back in his life. I had to break his gaze and turn away. "Don't forget when we went back to Bemidji years later, and I proposed to you on that bridge."

There was no way I could forget about that day. It was the best day of my life. It was September, my favorite time of year. The trees were still in full bloom before they changed. We walked through the familiar path to the bridge and he got down on one knee. I had to rest my arms on the railing on the bridge to steady myself as he asked me to be his wife. I couldn't imagine my life without him, so I said, "Yes." I was sure I was glowing.

"Remember how mad Casey got that we hung out," he said. The mention of his name made me ill.

"I do."

"You sure played hard to get at first."

"I had to play the game, I didn't want to scare you away. I miss how we ran every morning together that year. I couldn't get enough of you," I said.

"I couldn't get enough of you either. As for Casey, he got over it and you two became better friends than him and me."

"I don't know about that," I said. "I couldn't believe Bryan Fredrickson could be interested in me. I knew I had to become friends with Casey or we would never last."

"And look at us now. We had a rough patch, but we are

getting through it and we will be stronger I just know it. I can't believe we will have a baby."

Should I tell him the truth? Will he forgive me? No, he would never forgive me, I know, because I couldn't forgive myself.

CHAPTER 5

JULY 1991

"Good morning, Mr. Fredrickson," I said as soon as his eyes opened.

"Good morning. Now this I can get used to," he said. A big smile spread across his face. He rolled onto his side and stared at me. His head rested on his open hand. With his other hand, he ran his thumb down my jaw line, sending chills throughout my body.

"God, have I missed you." He pulled down the sheets a little and looked up at me. Lifting my shirt just enough to expose my expanding belly, he put his hand on my stomach and began to softly rub it.

"I never thought I'd be so excited to have a baby bump," I said, meeting his gaze.

"Hello, baby girl. It's me, your daddy again. I can't wait to meet you, just hopefully not too soon. We want you to be healthy, you little soccer player." As if in response, little Gabriella kicked, exposing a small lump in my belly.

We both laughed, and he leaned in to kiss it. He sat up and kissed my forehead before getting up and pulling on his pants.

"Do you really have to go to work already?" I said, looking at the clock.

"Oh, I would much rather stay in bed with you all day, but someone has to keep the streets safe. Would you like to join me for a shower?" He grabbed his uniform off the hanger in the closet. Bryan perfectly pressed it. He hated wrinkles, and he loved to iron. Sometimes he would even iron his socks because he said that made him feel like they were brand new. So does a little bleach, honey. Of course, I just shook my head at his goofy OCD routines.

"I would love to, but the third trimester isn't treating me any better than the first two. I have to sit in bed and eat these saltines before I can even get up to pee," I said, reaching for the box of crackers on the nightstand.

"I'm sorry you are still sick. Is there anything I can do?"

"No, I'll be okay. At this rate, I may not even fit in the bathroom next week. How can I be so big when all I do is puke all day?"

"Because our baby is still growing. The doctor said your morning sickness should go away soon."

"I don't think they should consider it morning sickness when I am sick all day from morning to night. I dunno how women do it while working full time."

"Get some rest, honey. If you need anything, I am only a phone call away."

I sat in bed and fought the acid rising up. I chewed slowly, careful not to upset my stomach even more. My body was so heavy to lift and I could no longer even tie my shoes. How was I going to make it through another month or more like this? I forced myself to get up and join him in the shower, anyway.

Dropping my clothes on the bathroom floor, I opened up the curtain to see his naked body and perfect curves as he stared back at me, smiling. His eyes scanned my body from head to toe, leaving me feeling self-conscious as he raised his eyebrows in approval. I stepped in front of him as he put his arms around my belly and pulled me in as close as he could for a kiss.

He tried to slide past me so I could get under the warm water, but we both broke out in laughter because there was no way he could get around me without getting out of the shower completely. My belly was too big and the bathtub too small.

"Well, I guess I will just have to move the water." He adjusted the shower head and moved back so I could warm up.

I let the water run down my back as he bent over to grab the shampoo. I could hear the air squirting out into his hand from the bottle. He pulled my shoulders back and massaged it into my hair. I relaxed, feeling a little unbalanced, and closed my eyes. His hands ran down my back, his fingers dragging against my skin, which gave me goosebumps.

I put my head back into the water to wash it out. He reached around me and ran his fingers over my belly. I moved my hands down and put my hands on top of his.

"Do you feel that?"

"Yeah, it's amazing. Does it hurt at all when she kicks like that?"

"No, although it feels weird. Can you believe we will have a baby girl in a few weeks?"

"I can't wait," he said.

My hands squeezed his bulging arms and slid down his bare back. He felt so good, so soft, so perfect. The guilt hit me and I instantly felt sad, ruining this whole moment with him with thoughts of what I did.

"I have to go to work. I love you," he said, pulling me in for another kiss.

I finished washing my hair by myself and toweled off. I looked at myself in the full-length mirror and scowled at my reflection. Who had I become? I put on my t-shirt and slipped into bed as the exhaustion hit me. All I could do was sleep these days.

MY PHONE RANG and woke me from a sound sleep. It was the best sleep I'd had in week

"Hello," I said, groggily.

"Why, hello there? Dez?"

"Who is this?"

"I hear congratulations are in order. It's Casey. You don't remember my voice anymore?"

I sat up a little, placing a pillow under my lower back and grabbing a saltine.

"Casey, why are you calling me? Where have you been? Bryan has been worried sick."

"Well, after my dad passed, I just needed to get away for a while. My mom and I went to Europe for a couple months and I come back to find my best friends, whom I thought were getting a divorce, are having a baby."

"I take it you talked to Bryan."

"Yes, he sounds very happy. Now the real question is, are you happy?"

I sat there for a moment, unsure of how to answer. "Yes, Casey, I am. I love him."

He cleared his throat. "You do, huh? Are you sure about that?"

I felt sick to my stomach and frozen, unable to say a word back.

"He's too good for you, you know that," he said.

I cupped my hand around my mouth, not understanding how to respond to that. I hoped he would hang up. I couldn't believe he came back. Why? I wanted him to go away again, far, far away.

"I know he is. If you are trying to hurt me it isn't working."

"You made me a promise. Now I will have to follow through with mine," he said, sending chills down my spine.

"No, please don't, please," I pleaded, dropping the phone to the ground. I lost all control as the tears continued.

He had to be lying to me, he just had to be. How could he do this? He wouldn't tell him, would he?

CHAPTER 6

My feet and hands swelled as the pregnancy progressed. Bryan gave me foot massages while I laid in bed and read almost every night. As my belly expanded that last trimester, I gained my tiger stripes. He thought they were cute and told me I got them because I was such a warrior. Sometimes he would kiss them and then rub them with vitamin E, while singing to the baby. Although Bryan's shifts were constantly changing, we never missed a run together. Every day we found time to push each other to move, enjoying Minnesota seasons. One day we went running, and it was fifty below outside and we literally ran around the block and came home with icicles hanging from our eyelashes. We ran as far as we could every day, depending upon how I was feeling. The doctor said it was okay for me to run as long as I listened to my body.

Casey called a couple times to meet us for dinner, but I told Bryan to go without me both times. I said I wasn't feeling good, and he said he understood. Every day I was on edge, wondering if he would tell Bryan. I came to realize his promise was more of a threat. He wanted to control me, but I didn't understand why.

I WALKED into the nursery to enjoy my baby girl's bedroom Bryan and I had finally finished, after weeks of hard work and long hours. I took in each detail with a smile, imagining what it will be like when she is born.

I picked up the soft teddy bear that laid in the new white rocking chair. Sitting down, I placed the bear behind my aching lower back. I rested my hands on my belly and smiled, taking in the scenery.

"Hello baby Gabriella. I can't wait to finally hold you in my arms. I just pray you are a healthy baby." I stared out the window and saw Bryan's car pull into the driveway.

"Oh, baby girl," I said while rubbing my big bulging stomach. "What am I doing being a mom? Sometimes I wonder how this all happened so fast. I love you and I promise to always be there for you, no matter what life brings our way."

I sang a lullaby and rock in the chair, imagining holding her in my arms. A shadow caught my eye and Bryan's head peeked around the door.

"Hey baby, what ya doin'?" He took a few steps into the bedroom and looked around. He shook his head and smiled at me. He pulled a bouquet of yellow lilies out from behind his back.

"Oh, they are beautiful, thank you," I said, getting up with the help of his hand. I could not believe little things like tying my shoe or getting out of a chair or the car could be so difficult. I felt like a big fat penguin and waddled like one too. He pulled me in for a hug.

"I'm just having a little one-on-one with Gabby."

"I'm sad I missed it."

"Our little pea just kicked me," I said.

He bent down so his face was inches from my swollen belly.

"Hey there Gabby, are you going to be a soccer player or are you just trying to tell me mama belongs to you?" As if replying, the baby kicked just inches from Bryan's face and we both erupted in laughs.

"I'm not sure why you keep calling her a pea. Do you not notice my belly is the size of a hot air balloon?"

He stood up and stared into my eyes. "You are more beautiful today then you were yesterday," he said. "Who knew that was possible?"

"Oh, Bryan," I said. "Thank you but I don't believe a word."

And then he kissed me.

I WENT into labor around three in the morning. By seven I was at the hospital and Gabriella Irene Fredrickson was born. She was eight pounds, three and a half ounces. She had a full head of curly hair that fell out two days later and grew back in ringlets. I decided not to have any drugs and Bryan was by my side through it all. He was my focal point as we breathed together through every contraction. I had a twelve-minute delivery, which my doctor said was phenomenal. I expected her cry to be louder than it was and I could not understand why people complained about screaming babies so much. We were a great team, Bryan and I.

We focused on Gabby, who was growing into a sweet little girl and probably a little too spoiled. We had our struggles, but we focused so much on baby Gabby, we never stopped to think about ourselves or our relationship. We took turns going out with our friends so one of us would be home to babysit. We did not realize we were setting up our marriage for failure because we did not get enough time together.

My mom helped when she could, but I needed her while I finished up my Associate's Degree. Bryan worked a lot to support us and had to sleep during the day after he worked midnights.

I realized involving my mom, the alcoholic, in my life wasn't the best idea. Although she was sober during the day when she had Gabby, she was constantly trying to tell us what we were doing wrong and how we should raise our child. Her way was the only way.

One time my mom gave Gabby a Baby Asprin when she was just two. I told her Baby aspirins were not actually for babies and she stormed off and wouldn't talk to me for a week. Another time, she gave Gabby a peanut butter sandwich at just thirteen months. Oh, I was so mad because I was told by doctors to wait until she was at least two just in case she was allergic. She told me what I should or shouldn't do, and if I told her Gabby was too young, she would shrug her shoulders and say, "I fed you and your sister that and you two are just fine." What I wanted for my child didn't matter. Mom demanded she got her way, or she'd punish me for days.

Bryan's parents were just very supportive, and I was much closer to them than my mom. I began distancing myself from her and gravitating toward Bryan's family.

Casey came around way too often after the baby was born. It strained my relationship with Bryan when he was around, because I felt so guilty.

Every day my relationship with Bryan got a little weaker. We didn't really give each other much attention. We were constantly fighting over what was the punishment when Gabby colored on the wall or when Gabby hit a kid on the playground, or when she flushed a washcloth down the toilet, flooding the bathroom. Bryan would laugh and I would get angry.

We took all of our anger out on each other and I began making a habit out of slamming the door when we fought and locking myself in my room. He would become silent and eventually got around to apologizing to me, even if I was the one in the wrong. I no longer apologized, and Bryan no longer blamed me for our fights. I became spoiled, always getting my way, beginning to hate who I'd become. Bryan just kept on fighting for me by taking the fault.

We tried not to argue in front of Gabby, but as she got older she caught on. By her fifth birthday, we no longer slept in the same bed or kissed. Bryan would try, but I would just pull away. We lost that spark we once had, and I gave up on us.

CHAPTER 7

JANUARY 1997

*H*earing a knock at the door, I put down the dish towel to answer it. Casey.

"Hey Dez, everything okay?" He had concern in his eyes as he handed me a bouquet of roses. I turned around and threw them in the garbage.

"You can drop the act, Casey, Bryan isn't here yet."

He reached into the garbage, pulling out the flowers.

"I'm sorry about what I said, Dez. I guess I was just upset at the news. I was in shock. I was scared you would tell him, so I threatened you. Please forgive me. What happened is the past, and I will never tell him. Cross my heart." He smiled at me, his perfect teeth and sincere smile made me want to just move past all of this.

"Never talk to me like that again. The only reason I'm letting this go is because you haven't told him yet. You've definitely had infinite opportunities." I glared, pouring us both a glass of Merlot. I was glad Gabby was staying at Judy and Carl's tonight.

"Thank you. I will be better, scout's honor." He pulled out a stool at the breakfast bar and sat down, putting up the girl scout sign with three fingers. I just laughed to myself. He slid out the stool next to him for me. I handed him a glass and set the bottle in between us on the counter.

"To a better start to our new friendship." With that, we clanked our glasses, and I gulped down the entire glass and poured myself another.

Casey stared at me in shock. "Listen, I want to make it up to you."

"Oh, really, and how are you going to do that?"

"Well, Bryan told me you are sick of staying home all the time, so I thought maybe you would like to come work at the firm."

"You want me to come and work for you? I don't think that's a very good idea, Casey. Plus, I don't want to work full-time."

"Just hear me out. Sophia just put in her two weeks Thursday because she is going to law school. Jim and I have been interviewing, but we just can't find what we are looking for. Would you be interested in a legal assistant position? The pay would be around ten dollars an hour starting off and you would mainly do secretarial work, but it would be a great experience for the time being."

"I dunno, Casey. I don't think us working together is a very good idea." I felt a bit of excitement at the idea, but still had my doubts if I would enjoy doing that kind of work. Also, the thought of working with Casey gave me a bit of anxiety. Although what happened between us was in the past, I still felt guilty and uncomfortable alone with him. He scared me.

"The job would start off at thirty hours a week, eight to

two. Jim's wife, Linda, comes in right now from two to five to give Sophia a break and she is really enjoying working there, but full-time is too much for her. If you stay, you could go up to forty hours a week and Linda would probably just come in and do some filing after you leave. She likes to make sure the office is organized. She is a retired secretary for some dentist's office and likes to take care of the place a little as a hobby to keep herself busy."

"I'll think about it," I replied, getting up to take the cherry cheesecake out of the fridge. I put it down, licking my fingers.

"Don't worry about our past, it will stay in the past. Destiny, it was one night that we both regret. We promised to start over. Just come work for us until you find something else. At least come in for an interview." He was right, I needed to try to move past this.

"I will think about it."

"Will you at least talk to Bryan about it?"

I sat there, taking it all in. It didn't sound so bad. I wouldn't mind having a desk job, dressing nicely again. Then again, could I stand to work for Casey? I checked on the chicken breasts in the oven and cut one open, not pink. I took them out, cut them up and began mixing them in with the rice when I heard the door shut. Within a couple seconds, Bryan was at my side, his lips planted on my cheek.

"Smells delicious."

"It's just chicken and rice, but thank you." I picked up the pan and put it on a hot pad on the table. When I turned around his arms were open. I hated when he wanted to touch me in that uniform. He needed a shower.

"Bryan, go change before you touch me." It came out of my mouth a little ruder than I had expected, but no reason to apologize at this point. He went into the living room, said hello to Casey and headed upstairs for a quick shower.

He returned in an old hockey shirt and jeans. He went into the living room to chat with Casey before I called them both in to eat. I kept the chicken and rice warm in the oven while finishing up the peas in the microwave. I took the aluminum foil off the food and grabbed some rice and chicken before passing it to Casey and reaching for the peas on the counter.

"So, Casey was telling me there is an opening for a secretary position at his law office. Did he happen to mention it to you at all? I thought it would be perfect for you," he said, smiling. He put down the chicken and rice and looked my way, clasping his fork in his right hand.

I looked over at Casey and glared. "Yeah, he mentioned it."

"And, what do you think? Just for the time being?" he said, looking hopeful.

"You would be perfect for it, Dez," Casey added.

I tried to read Casey, tried to figure out if this was another trick. How could I turn it down in front of Bryan when all I'd been doing lately was complaining about not being able to find a part-time job.

"I dunno, I'll think about it."

"What's there to think about? You'd be perfect for the job. Unless there is some reason why you'd feel uncomfortable working there," Casey said with an innocent look on his face.

I shot him a giant smile, "Maybe I would like to work there. When can I start?"

I knew I needed to get him off my back, fast. No way was he going to start this again. He had something up his sleeve. The rest of the dinner I sat in silence and listened to them go on about the Vikings. I couldn't wait to get Bryan alone. The guilt was eating at me and I had a great idea of what I wanted to do to him after Casey left. I knew what would make him smile, and he deserved to be happy. I love him.

Casey and Bryan cleaned up the kitchen after dinner, while I went and took a hot bath. It was tradition when Casey came for dinner, the boys always did the dishes while I relaxed. Bryan insisted, because I worked hard making the meal.

When I got out of the bath, I noticed the light was off in the downstairs hallway, so I knew Casey had left. I decided I would put on my lacy red teddy, that didn't leave much for the imagination, and go down to the basement and crawl in bed with him. I needed to try harder, show him how I really felt. I needed to stop the darkness that crept above my head most days and try to let him in.

Since Gabby was at a sleepover at my in-laws, I decided on the matching see-through thong, thigh-high pantyhose, and red high heels. I walked down the stairs and noticed the bathroom light was on. I leaned against the hallway and did my sexiest pose. It had been weeks since we had any fun and I was so excited to surprise him. I heard the water turn off and the bathroom door opened quickly, the light above me in the hallway shined like a spotlight.

"Hey baby, want to take me into your dungeon?" I said in my sexiest voice as the door cracked open and there stood Casey with wide eyes and his mouth hanging open. "Oh my god, Casey?" I could feel the heat from my face blending in with my teddy. "I... I..." I stood there, frozen.

He laughed at me and put his fist over his mouth.

"I thought... you were... gone," I mumbled, covering up my chest as much as possible and with another hand covering up my tiny thong. I turned around and ran upstairs with one hand covering my bottom.

Casey laughed. "No thank you," he said, walking out the door.

I was so embarrassed. No way could I tell Bryan what just

happened. I laid my head on my pillow after I stripped my teddy off and cried. The guilt was eating me alive. Why did I accept the job working for this jackass? I would give it a couple weeks, then start applying for other jobs; no way would he trap me there.

CHAPTER 8

I walked into my new office Monday morning and was greeted by a beautiful brunette. "You must be Destiny," she said, shaking my hand with a huge grin. "I'm Sophia."

"Hello, Sophia." I felt guilty and ill to be here, but it was only a couple weeks, I reminded myself.

"You can hang your jacket up on the hook in the corner, behind your desk and your purse can go in the bottom of that file cabinet," she said, pointing.

I put my things away and sauntered back to the desk she just sat down at.

"So, I have a few basic things to show you before Casey takes you out for coffee."

I felt sick. "Wait a minute, why is Casey taking me to coffee? I mean, I just got here."

"He always takes the new assistants to the cafe and tells them about expectations within the company. It is nothing to worry about, I promise," she reassured me. "I must admit, I was a little worried they wouldn't find anyone to replace me in time. I only have one more day left here. My orientation starts Wednesday, can you believe it?" she said, too peppy for this moment.

"Wait a minute, I only have one more day of training with you?" I blurted out. I couldn't believe it. There was no way that was enough time for me to learn everything.

"Yeah, but don't worry," she shot back, placing a hand on my shoulder, "Jim is out most of the week on a trial, but Casey only has felony court tomorrow and will be around the rest of the week to help you. He sounds very confident you will do just fine." She smiled, turning to her computer to explain how to run the answering machine, answer the phone, and explain where the files are kept for public defendant and private clients.

She opened a private folder and showed me the file's outline. She explained how public defendant files were put together a bit differently than the rest, and all the paperwork was labeled and clipped to the right side. She went through the billing system briefly and told me Casey would be out of his office at ten o'clock sharp for coffee.

By ten, I was so overloaded with information, but I couldn't stop watching for him to open up his office. He was a half hour late, and I hoped he had forgotten about me; I couldn't be so lucky.

"I am so sorry for the wait, Destiny, Jim was having some issues finding some paperwork for his trial, but they were just in the wrong order. Shall we?" He put his arm out for me to clasp and walked me out.

"No problem. Sophia was just telling me she will only be here one more day and then you will train me. Funny you didn't mention this bit of information earlier." I felt anxious at the thought. I was nervous about working in the office, even if being fired wasn't the worst thing that could happen to me. The worst thing is being trapped here with him, alone. Casey watching me, correcting my every move.

"I knew you could handle it. It is my job to be by your side at all times; now let's go."

He led me out of the office and down the stairs to the small but comfortable coffee shop.

"What can I get for you? It's on the house."

"Aren't you the best boss ever," I retorted.

"Funny, I hear that all the time," he responded, checking out the beautiful petite Italian barista. "One French vanilla cappuccino and the usual for me." She blushed at him as he handed her his credit card, and it disgusted me.

I could see right through this jerk and was sorry she couldn't. He acted like a powerful junior attorney. Why should she fear him? Poor girl had no clue what he was capable of. I shook the thought away. Focus.

A few moments later, we both grabbed our coffee and the barista, with the name tag Adreana, just stared at Casey. We headed back to the table and a laugh escaped his lips.

"What is so funny?" I asked, confused.

"I was just thinking about the look on your face when you saw it was me and not your husband coming out of the bath-room." I instantly blushed in anger.

"Casey, this isn't the time," I replied, coldly.

"I'm sorry, I just haven't been able to get you off my mind since that night." Mocking me, he looked down at his coffee and took another sip.

"Let's just not speak of this again. It was hard enough accepting a job with you when I can't even trust you. I just want you to promise me that if you told Bryan our secret, you will talk to me first. You owe me that, at least. I want to tell him, but I just can't break his heart yet. I mean, if Bryan found out--"

"Dez, he will not find out," he snapped. "I do not want to break up my friendship with him over a stupid mistake. But you know you are beautiful. Since we will never talk about that night again after this, I just want you to know you were amazing," he said. I knew he was crossing the line, but I decided to just let it go. I just wanted it all to go away.

"As long as you aren't trying to play me. I can't believe I have to run the office by myself in just a couple days. This is crazy."

"It will be fine. If you wouldn't have started so soon, I would run the office by myself until we found someone. I know how smart you are. You will catch on in no time, I promise, just relax." He placed his hand on mine and it took everything out of me not to punch him in the face.

As I came back from the bathroom, the barista was talking to him at the table. She handed him a piece of paper and he gave it back to her, apologizing. What was wrong with him? Why wouldn't he take her number? I rolled my eyes and headed back to the table. I couldn't wait to get away from him.

"WELL, how was your first day at work?" Bryan greeted me with a big hug when I walked in the door. I felt a little guilty and anxious about having to work with Casey.

"It was fine. I mean, it's just for a little while, right? It is a lot of information, but nothing I can't figure out."

"I'm glad it was a good day, babe," he said, putting on his uniform. "Your day is over and now mine begins. Gabby is in her room reading Spot books. She is really doing a good job of sounding out the words." He kissed me on the forehead, then headed to the door. He turned around and came back to me.

"Well, my first day of afternoons. Don't forget, Friday I have to double-out for George. He's going to the Bahamas with his wife. We should definitely do something like that someday. Love ya," he said, kissing me goodbye.

Gabby and I spent the night reading together and playing Barbies before she got into the shower. She didn't like baths and told me they were for babies and she was five, so she was too old for baths. She was five going on thirteen.

I laid on my stomach, face down into my pillow. I let out a muffled scream into it. Should I really work with Casey after what we did to Bryan? Maybe we should tell Bryan. Maybe I should just leave Bryan for good. I didn't deserve to be with him after what I did. The pain in my stomach was never going to go away until I could be honest. I knew what I had to do. I got up and went to pick out some pajamas for Gabby. As I stepped into the hall, the phone on the wall rang.

"Hello?"

"Hey Dez, it's Casey."

I couldn't speak.

"Do you want to go out with Jim and me Friday night? We want to celebrate the new addition to our company."

I sat there, silent, unable to respond.

"Hello, are you there?" he snapped.

"I'm here."

"And Dez, bring Bryan with you. We will be there to pick you up around seven."

He never even gave me time to respond before he hung up the phone. That bastard. I needed to come up with a good excuse. What did he want from me?

CHAPTER 9

*W*ednesday Morning was my first day without Sophia. I walked in, put my jacket away and sat at my desk, twenty minutes early. I looked at the pile of papers on my desk to file. Turning on some music, I began filing. I danced around, trying to shake out my nerves. I shook my hips and went through half the stack of papers before the phone rang. I turned down the volume on the radio and made my way to pick it up. As I turned around, I saw Casey watching me from the window in the hallway and felt the instant rosiness in my cheeks. I stood there in shock as he opened up the door.

His smiling face stared back at me. "Well, are you going to continue dancing around or answer the phone?" he teased.

"Oh, yeah, right," I responded, taking the last step to the phone. "Hello. Hello." I hung up the phone.

"Well?" he asked, raising his eyebrows and crossing his arms, briefcase in hand.

"They hung up."

"I'm not sure why," he said, rolling his eyes and heading into his office.

I was sure I would throw up. I debated following him into his office and apologizing, but continued filing with the music down more.

I finished up the filing just before Casey came out of his office and put another stack on my desk.

"These are letters I need you to write to clients about their upcoming court dates. Are you familiar with Windows 95?"

I did not understand what he was talking about. "No, not really. I used an Apple in school."

"Okay, here, let me show you," he said, moving me over and sitting down in my chair.

The next two hours he spent showing me how to use the computer and even typed up one of the client letters for me.

"Do you feel comfortable with this at all?" he asked.

"I don't know, I guess. I will just need to practice." I smiled, wondering if this job was too much for me. If maybe he was too much. I just wanted him to leave me alone now. I could always use the web to tell me what I needed to know about Windows.

As if some higher power was helping me escape from this conversation, the phone rang.

"Hello, Johnson Law Office, this is Destiny," I answered, feeling the sweat dripping from my forehead as Casey sat there judging me. "Yes he is, hang on. It's for you," I said, looking at Casey.

I held out the phone to him and he reached across me, brushing his arm against mine. I watched his finger touch the hold button.

"My first rule is, never ever say I am here. You always tell them I am on the other line right now and take a message on the notebook immediately. I can't believe Sophia didn't mention this to you," he said, shakily.

"I'm sorry, what do you want from me? I'll tell them whatever you want," I apologized, feeling shaky.

"Take a deep breath."

I took a breath and let it out quickly.

"Just tell them I am on the other line and take the message, please." He said, walking away and slamming his door shut.

I didn't see him again until around noon. I didn't want to apologize. It just made me work harder while he was gone. Every call after that, I took a message. When he walked out of his office, he acted as though nothing happened. Any moment, I was sure I would lose it.

"You hungry?" he asked. His body turned away from me while he pulled out a yellow legal pad from the cupboard.

"Kinda," I mumbled under my breath.

"Okay, I will get us some pizza. I'm sorry I got mad at you earlier, I have a lot on my mind. Don't take it personally."

Don't take it personally? Seriously?

HE CAME BACK with pepperoni slices for both of us about a half hour later.

"Come eat in my office with me, there is a table in there."

I followed him into his office and we sat right next to each other, against my better judgment.

"How is everything going, Dez? Did you get all the filing done today?"

"Well, there were a few names I couldn't find, but I just have to keep looking."

"Some files are stored because the cases are closed. I will look at them and let you know. You can just put them in a pile on my desk and I will show you where the closed files are located tomorrow."

"Okay," I answered, trying not to make direct eye contact with him.

"So, did you talk to Bryan about Friday yet?"

"He's working overtime and I don't have a sitter, maybe another night."

He rolled his eyes at me.

"I really am sorry I snapped at you earlier. Let me know if you change your mind. Did you experiment with AOL yet?"

"No, I haven't. I have used AOL before, though. Should I set up a new email for the office?" I asked, trying to keep our conversation professional.

Although I didn't have much of an appetite, the pizza gave me something to do with my hands. He made me feel so uncomfortable.

"Sophia already has one on the computer. You look so stressed out. Is everything okay at home?" he asked, eyeing me curiously.

"Yeah, it's fine. It's just really weird, you know, having you as my boss," I said, like I would tell him anything that was going on at home.

"It'll be fine."

I nodded, picking at my cheese. He got up, wiping his hands on his napkin.

"We couldn't just hire anyone for the job. I trust you. We have history."

The way he said it shot a shiver down my spine. He walked behind me and put his hands on my shoulders. I was afraid to move. He began rubbing them, but it was a little too hard and uncomfortable.

"You look a little tense, Dez. Let's not talk about work, let's talk about Bryan," he said, his fingers running up my neck.

"What about Bryan?" I snapped, trying to lean forward

and pull away, but his hands were too strong, holding me back.

"How are you two doing?"

"Um, okay," I said, my voice shaking. I was sitting with perfect, uncomfortably stiff posture.

"Let's get something straight. Do you want to continue working here?" His voice became powerful, deeper.

"I have been waiting for the catch."

"Well then, you need to leave Bryan," he ordered.

I stood up and turned around, not caring that my pizza flew right off my plate and onto my shoe and the white carpet in his office.

"Are you kidding me, Casey?"

He laughed and inched his way closer to me. I could feel his breath on my face. I didn't breath, in fear of smelling his foul breath again.

"No. Unless you want me to tell him you took advantage of me while I was drunk, you need to leave him."

I felt my body shaking. "What are you talking about? Why would you lie? Why do you want me to leave Bryan so bad?"

I closed my fists so he couldn't see how badly I was shaking with anger.

He slid the back of his hand down my face. I took a step back, slapping his hand off of me.

"Don't touch me!" I screamed.

"Oh, Dez. You are so cute when you are angry, you know that?"

"Why do you want me to leave him, Casey? Why? We are trying to work things out, I'm trying to be happy. What do you get out of me leaving Bryan?"

"You will do what I say. You have until Friday. Leave him or I will tell him the truth. Bryan can do so much better than you. I don't want to see him wasting his time with a lying bitch like you. Maybe you should have taken me up on our offer for Friday. You obviously don't trust me, so I don't trust you."

I felt the tears streaking my makeup down my face; the anger burning inside me; the walls closing in on me.

"But I love him! If I leave him, I will tell him about us. You can't stop me."

He remained calm as he once again leaned in, just inches from my face. "You don't want to mess with me."

"You don't scare me, Casey, I quit!" I screamed, pushing everything off his desk and onto the floor. I slammed his office door behind me, grabbing my coat and purse, running out the door before he could catch up with me. It terrified me, unsure of why he would do this to me. Was this a game? What could he gain from this plan? He'd lose Bryan too.

I slammed the door of my Oldsmobile and started it up. I loosened my short gray scarf with white stripes around my neck and pulled as hard as I could. I could feel it choking me as I struggled to free it from my neck with one hand. I finally got it off and threw it right out the window.

I began unbuttoning the button on my beige blazer as my car came to a halt in front of my house. I saw Bryan's truck parked in the driveway. I hit the top of the steering wheel with all my might. As I stepped out, I took off my blazer and threw it into my car. I was hot and sweating, wanting to take it all off the moment I got into my house. I felt suffocated by all of it. The clothes were fake, just like I had become. I walked in the door, taking off my grey stilettos and threw them across the floor, yelling out for Bryan.

A shadow followed me as I began unbuttoning my cashmere blouse. Then I turned around and saw the anger in his eyes. Frozen, my hand still holding on tight to the button. He knew. The fact that it exposed my bosoms as my white Victoria's Secret bra peeked out, didn't even bother me. His closed fists took aback me, tight jaw and eyes that could burn a hole right through me.

As he stepped into the light, I saw the red blotches on his forehead, his eyes swollen. He looked like he was in more pain than anger.

"Is it true?"

I bit down hard on my lip, unable to look him straight in the eyes.

"Destiny, is it true?" His voice got a little louder, a little angrier.

I looked down at the floor, crossing my arms. That asshole called already, got ahold of him before I could tell him myself.

"Yes."

His glare broke my heart, ate at my soul every second we sat there in silence until he finally continued. "Is Gabby...Is Gabby his?" he cried out, putting his hand in front of his mouth, terrified of my answer.

"Really? Is that what he said? No, no way. It was one time, months before we conceived her. I promise," I pleaded, taking a step toward him. Showing him the sadness, the aching in my heart.

He stepped back, putting out his hand to stop me from coming any closer. "Get out. Just get out."

"I'm so sorry, it only happened once, I promise." I pleaded.

"Get out. Get out now!" He screamed, making his way to the couch. "I can't even look at you right now. Not another word. When Gabby gets home from school, I will tell her you had to go on a training or something. You need to give me this," he said, too soft.

I made my way upstairs, packing a suitcase as I zoned out. I wasn't going back to the office with Casey, that I knew for sure. I packed a few outfits and my makeup. I pulled out the bobby pins from my poof and pulled out my black banana clip and replaced it with a thin scrunchie. I threw on a baby-T with a peace sign, and a pair of jeans, and made my way down the stairs, scared to see him again.

"I love you," I whispered to his back, unsure if he could even hear me.

CHAPTER 10

"What would ever drive you to jump in bed with that man, Dez?"

"That's the thing, Jill, I don't even remember it. I just woke up in bed with him, naked. I must have blocked it out of my mind or blacked out or something." I tried remembering the night in my head, like I had tried to do so many times, but I still couldn't remember having sex with him.

"So, he stopped over after his dad died and you ended up in bed with him?" Her voice was just pissing me off.

"Jill, it was innocent, I promise. He came over to see Bryan. He didn't know he wouldn't be home. I honestly have absolutely no feelings for Casey, never have. I mean, he was a friend, and in college I thought he was a jerk and was only nice to him because he was best friends with Bryan. I woke up in the morning sick to my stomach when I realized what I had done. It was horrible."

"Sounds like the night you ended up in bed with your husband. You know, the night you conceived Gabby. You just ended up in bed with him, pissed off the next morning," she mocked me, rolling my eyes.

"It isn't the same, Jill. I remember what happened that night with Bryan. I mean, not at first, but it slowly came to me. What happened with Casey was different. I remember having a drink with him, but nothing after that."

"Maybe you erased it from your mind on purpose. I've heard of that happening before," she said, adding half a stick of butter to the mashed potatoes she was putting in the microwave.

"It doesn't even matter anymore. We are over. Done. Casey's an ass. How could he do this? Do you think Bryan will still be friends with him after that?"

"I don't know. I really don't know. I mean, I can't believe Casey had the balls to call him. I really don't understand why he wanted you to leave Bryan so bad. What does he get out of it, anyway? Maybe he is jealous and wants him all to himself."

"Stop with the jokes, Jill. This isn't funny, this is my life."

Her kitchen phone began ringing, but neither of us moved to answer it. We let her answering machine pick it up.

"Jill, it's Carl. I can't seem to get ahold of Destiny."

Jill and I exchanged glances, neither one of us moving to pick up the phone.

"There has been an accident. If you talk to Destiny, tell her to meet us at the hospital, it's Bryan."

We both raced across the kitchen to pick up the phone, but he had already hung up. I couldn't believe what I had just heard.

"An accident? Oh no, his parents don't have a cell phone. Rewind it Jill, rewind it!"

Jill rewound the cassette and played it again as I ran across her kitchen floor, grabbing my jacket, keys and purse off the kitchen table. I slipped my wooden clogs on and we both ran out to my car, Jill trailing slightly behind me.

"Dez, let me drive. I don't think you should be driving," she called out to me.

I didn't have time to argue with her. I threw her my keys, and she caught them, slipping in the driver's seat and slamming the door behind her. I grabbed my Nokia—1610 version with a small antenna, made for talking only—off the seat. I had a missed call too, but they didn't leave a message on my phone.

Jill drove fast, I'm not sure how fast because it was all a blur. We reached the emergency room, and I just ran as fast as I could. I didn't realize I was crying until I reached the lady behind the counter in the emergency room.

"I'm looking for Bryan Fredrickson. He is here, I think. He was in an accident."

"Calm down, let me see what I can find out. Who are you, ma'am?" She spoke calmly, too calmly. She didn't seem to care that I was distraught.

"I'm his wife," I said, my voice shaking. How could she not know that?

She got up and walked away without another word. I turned around, paced the waiting room. My heart felt like it would explode.

"Calm down," Jill whispered, pulling me in for a hug.

I pushed her away, leaned over the counter to search for the woman.

"Destiny?" I heard from behind me.

I saw Bryan's parents and ran to hug them. They were in tears, our bodies trembling together.

"Where is Bryan? Is he okay? What happened?"

"They just took him by ambulance to Duluth, Dez. He's —" Carl said, holding my hands.

"Oh my god, is he going to be okay? What happened? What happened?"

"He was on his way to pick up Gabby, he was on the highway and he went through a red light. He...he's hurt bad. They didn't tell us much. We need to get to Duluth right away. They are taking him to St. Mary's, his condition is too serious for Hibbing to handle."

I didn't want to hear any more. I grabbed Jill's arm and the next thing I knew I was racing across the parking lot.

"Slow down, slow down. I'm driving."

"This is all my fault. If I wouldn't have done what I did, this wouldn't of happened."

"It will be all right, Dez, this isn't your fault. Listen to me, it's not your fault, ya hear me?"

I just ignored her as my sobs grew louder and my heart began beating faster. It's all my fault, it's all my fault, I kept repeating over and over in my head.

As we pulled up to the hospital, Jill dropped me off so she could park the car. I didn't even wait for the car to come to a complete stop before I was running at full speed to the nearest information desk. I had no idea where he would be. I slowed down to glance down both halls, searching for a nurse.

I saw the information sign and the desk beneath it. I ran as fast as I could, unable to stop at this speed, and crashed my abdomen into the counter. I didn't even feel the pain as it knocked the wind out of me. I struggled to talk.

"I'm looking for my husband, Bryan Fredrickson. An ambulance took him here, he was in a car accident, where would he be?"

The panic in my voice made her talk faster in response.

"If he was taken by ambulance, he should be on the health trauma neuro floor, located down the hall to the left. There is a big sign, you can't miss it." She talked fast, but I remembered every word. I slowed down so I wouldn't miss it. Entering the doors, I saw a waiting room and another desk.

"Excuse me, my husband is here, I think he is here. Bryan Fredrickson? He was in a car accident."

She didn't react as though it was an emergency like the last lady, she took her time looking through some papers.

"How long ago did he get here?" she asked.

"I dunno. Probably not very long ago. I mean, I don't know, I just got a call and—"

"Slow down, slow down. I can't understand you if you talk that fast. Why don't you have a seat and I will let you know as soon as I find anything out? Why don't you fill out this paperwork. There is nothing you can do right now. You just need to stay calm. Are you his wife?"

"Yes, why does everyone keep asking me that?" I tried to calm myself down, but what I wanted to do was punch this blonde in the face. My husband is here somewhere, and I needed answers.

"Please sit down ma'am and let us do our job. There is nothing you can do for him right now. I promise, as soon as I find anything out, I will let you know." With that, she got up and walked into the closed doors behind her that read, Employees Only.

Sitting down in the chair, my leg shook, making it hard to even read the paperwork. I began tapping the top of the pen on the clipboard she gave me, imagining him lying dead in a hospital bed. What would Gabby do if she lost her dad? Why did I do what I did? How can this be happening? It's all my fault. I rested my hand under my chin and continued tapping the pen on the clipboard when I wasn't writing until I saw Jill run in with Carl and Judy right behind her.

"Did you hear anything? Do you know how Bryan is?" Judy asked, looking as though she was on the verge of a nervous breakdown.

"The lady will find out and let us know. She wanted me to

fill out this paperwork," I said, pointing to the papers in my lap.

I reached into my purse and retrieved our insurance cards so I could finish filling it out. I wanted to distract myself from thinking about him. I looked up and saw Judy biting her nails and Carl looking nervously at the ground. Jill put her hand on my knee and squeezed it lightly, shooting me a nervous smile.

"You okay? Need any help with that?"

I shook my head and put my head back into the paperwork. I almost didn't see the woman coming back to the desk and calling out to me. Judy tapped on my shoulder to get my attention, and the four of us made our way quickly to the desk.

"The doctor is with him right now. It sounds like your husband hit his head hard and only has a slight gash on his forehead, which they are stitching up right now. They need to do some tests because the doctor wants to make sure there is no swelling in his brain, or other severe injuries. You won't hear anything for a little while, so why don't you guys follow me into the family waiting area where it is a little more comfortable. Are you all done with the paperwork?"

I nodded my head at her as I scanned the paperwork again to see if I missed anything. I handed her the clipboard before we followed her down the hall.

"There is a television in the corner, fresh coffee and cookies, and a pay phone right outside the door if you need it. If you are going anywhere, please let me know so we aren't looking for you."

"Okay," I mumbled, sitting down in a chair.

It felt like days before the doctor finally came in to talk to us. He shut the door behind him as he walked in.

"Mrs. Fredrickson?" he called out, unsure of who I was.

"Yes," I said, standing up to shake his hand.

"I am here to give you an update. As you know, he was in a terrible car accident and hit his head. The brain is about three point four pounds of delicate, soft tissue floating in fluid within the skull. Under the skull, there are three layers of membrane that cover and protect his brain. The brain tissue is soft and therefore can be compressed, pulled, and stretched. He missed a stop light and tried to swerve to miss a car which resulted in his car hitting a tree. The impact when he hit the tree caused his brain to move around inside his skull, which resulted in a slight swelling to his brain."

I put my hands up over my nose and mouth, waiting to find out what that meant exactly.

"It is a closed head injury, so the contents inside his head have not broken through, which is good," he explained, nodding his head to reassure me. "His brain just moved so fast it collided with the bony skull around it in a jarring movement, which bruised his brain tissue. We are unsure of how long he lost consciousness, but I can tell you his CT showed very small swelling. We will know more when he wakes up and we will be continuing to do CT's to see if the swelling is getting any worse. It is a lot of waiting. At this time, it does not look like the swelling is severe enough where it has no place to go, so right now it doesn't look like he will need surgery. He has a gash on his forehead we had to close with six stitches, but he was lucky. We will just have to monitor him and watch him over the next couple of days. Do you have questions for me?"

"Could this affect his memory at all?" I asked, trying to take this all in.

"It could. I mean, there is really no way to tell until he wakes up. It could affect his fine motor skills, I have known it to affect personalities, we really don't know right now. Do you have any other questions?"

"Yes, when can we see him?" Judy asked, stepping closer to the doctor.

"We will put him in the ICU, so just one person at a time, please. One of you can come with me right now."

I looked at Judy, and she nodded to me to go ahead.

"It's okay Judy, you go first." Although I was worried about him and wanted to see him, I was afraid that he wouldn't want to see me when he woke up. I felt guilty because a part of me wanted him to lose his memory of the last twenty-four hours, so he could forget I slept with his best friend and everything would be back to normal.

"Are you sure?"

I nodded.

"Here, call Donna. She picked up Gabby when this all happened, and Gabby will stay at her house tonight. Here's her number. I am sure she is wondering what is going on," she said, handing me a piece of paper with a number written on it.

"Thanks, Judy. I'm glad she's with Donna tonight, she just loves her."

Bryan's sister, Donna, loved Gabby like her own. I walked into the hallway and threw up in the garbage outside the door before pulling my cell phone out of my jacket.

CHAPTER 11

*G*abby's innocence made it harder for me to hold it all together. I crouched down in the hallway, back against the wall, hands covering my face.

"Are you okay?" The sound of my sister's voice helped me to my feet.

"No. What if he doesn't want to see me, Jill?"

She put her arm around me. "It will be okay. He will forgive you, just give it time. He needs you right now. Don't put all of this on your shoulders, you made a mistake."

"No, Jill, he won't forgive me. Life is too short, I know that now. I took it all for granted, let my marriage slowly slip away. For what? For years I punished myself, pulling away from him for what I did. Jill, I love him, this is what I was afraid of," I cried out, tears flowing down my face.

"You can make it right. What happened to Bryan is horrible, but at times like this, we truly realize what is important to us," she reassured me, patting my back.

"I took him for granted, ruined the time we had together. I ruined our family."

"Dez, you need to stop feeling sorry for yourself, stop

69

wishing you could change the past. All you can do is focus on the future and be there for him. You need to be strong for both Bryan and Gabby. Do you think you can do that?"

Looking up at the ceiling, I focused on blinking away my tears and wiping my eyes. I let out a deep sigh.

"Yeah, I can do that."

She took my hand and led me back into the waiting room, where we sat and waited for Judy to come back. Carl was there, staring, not saying a word.

THE DOOR OPENED, Judy's puffy eyes stared back at me.

"He's awake," she muttered.

I stood up.

"How is he?" Carl was the first to ask.

"He has a terrible headache and his blood pressure is low, but the doctor said he's doing well, considering. He has no recollection of the accident, but the doctor said that is to be expected. He was asking for you, Destiny."

I gave her a gentle hug before looking back at Jill, then followed Judy to Bryan.

"He's in through these doors, second curtain on the left."

I walked through the doors, peeking my head in the curtain to make sure it was him behind it. He was lying in the bed, eyes closed, a machine by his bedside. Closing the curtain slowly behind me, I inched my way closer to his bed.

I stared at his beautiful face and scruffy beard. My hand made its way on top of his and his eyes opened just as I touched him. He blinked a few times, struggling to flash me a smile. He grabbed my hand and squeezed it. His body suddenly grimaced in pain, his eyes pressed shut tightly, only a moan escaped from his lips.

"Bryan, are you okay? Would you like me to get someone?" I asked, letting go of his hand and brushing against his face gently.

"No, no, it's fine. I just have a horrible headache. Where's Gabby?"

"She's with Donna right now. Jill called my mom and she should get her in the morning. Gabby wanted to have a sleepover."

"I'm glad she isn't here."

"Listen, Bryan, I'm so sorry about what I did. It's been eating me alive for years. I mean, after I got the call that you were in an accident—I just never want to lose you, ever. I took our relationship for granted. I love you."

"Destiny, I love you too."

I smiled in disbelief, excitement filling my soul.

"Dez, I love you, but I just can't forgive you yet. I will need some time," he said, struggling to talk.

"I understand. I'll wait as long as you need me to. I love you so much. I almost lost you. I'm so sorry I wasn't there."

He grabbed my hand and squeezed his eyes shut again. "Dez, please go home and take care of Gabby. She needs you right now. Can you bring her to see me tomorrow? If I'm doing better?"

"But I want to stay here with you. I can't leave you," I pleaded.

"Dez, look at me," I struggled to meet his gaze. "Please, do this for me."

I could tell he was struggling to hold his eyes open, and I just wanted to make him happy, take his pain away.

"Okay, Bryan, I promise." I leaned in and kissed his forehead, slowly letting go of his hand.

"Thank you."

"Now get some rest. It's an order," I said, smiling.

He closed his eyes, and I wandered back down the hall to the waiting room.

"Well, how is he doing?" Jill asked, waiting right by the door when I walked in.

"He's doing okay. He needs some rest. Jill, would you mind bringing me home?"

"Are you leaving?" Judy asked, confused.

I walked over to where she was sitting, Carl's arm around her on the bright green waiting room chairs.

"Yes, Bryan and I think it is best for me to be with Gabby right now. Take care of him. Oh, and Judy, please keep me informed on his progress. No matter what time it is."

She stood up to hug me. "You know I will. Everything will be okay, I know it. Take care of yourself, Destiny."

"Jill, do you think our adult lives would be different if Dad would have been around and sober?"

"What do you mean? Like if Mom wouldn't have packed us up in the middle of the night to escape the alcohol, drugs, and constant beatings?" she asked, her voice full of anger. "Sorry, it still pisses me off."

"I get it. You were a lot older than I was at the time, so you remember it a lot better than I do."

"Yeah, well, you are lucky. I remember Mom shaking me awake, yelling at me to hurry. I could only bring a few small things that fit into my Rainbow Brite backpack and my teddy bear. I was six years old when we left. You were just a baby. Mom was crying, her black eye made me cry. Dad went out to get some more Vodka after he threw Mom's hot coffee in her face for not having a backup bottle," she said, staring at the road with a disgusted look on her face.

"I can't believe he did that. I never asked before, but is that when Mom became an alcoholic?"

"Yeah, not long after we moved here from California, she started drinking. She was afraid he would find us, so she numbed the anxiety with alcohol. There is just so much you don't know, Dez."

"I would like to know someday. Sometimes I just want to understand Mom, understand why she is so controlling and angry all the time. After all these years, she still won't get the help she needs. I guess I just don't get it. After what happened to Bryan, I realized that I want to be happy and I need to quit screwing everything up for myself. Sometimes I hear that voice in the back of my head, you know mom's voice. It's constantly telling me I'm not good enough, that I should fear everything in life. I just don't understand how she doesn't know she's an alcoholic."

"I am always worried dad will find Mom. Mom is scared and knows that if he finds her, he will probably kill her. What she did for us, by taking us out of that house and bringing us to Minnesota, was so brave. As for you, fight. Fight for Bryan, fight for your happiness. Fight for Gabby. That is something Mom did right. If she wouldn't of left, who knows what would have happened to us."

"That is exactly what I intend to do. I love him, Jill. I just pray for a quick recovery. Do you think Dad will ever find her, find us?" I asked, opening up the car door.

"I hope not. Hopefully, he is too drunk to find her."

CHAPTER 12

JANUARY 2017

I could hear them talking, but I couldn't see them. I saw flowers, a butterfly, beautiful rainbows covering the sky. I was running beside Bryan, enjoying the pounding our feet made as they hit the pavement in unison. The breeze tangled my hair and filled my lungs with energy, happiness. We continued running around the canyon, gazing over the side and laughing. Bryan held me close to loosen the constriction in my chest. He looked into my eyes and came closer, leaning in. As his lips touched mine, I felt the electric current, the earthquake that ripped at my heart again. The stomping sent me to my knees, and he was gone, just like that.

"The doctor said she will be awake less and less as the days go on. Although she made it through the surgery, there isn't much they can really do. We just have to pray for a miracle. He also said patients diagnosed with this have known for six months at the point she is at. He couldn't believe she didn't have any symptoms earlier."

I knew that voice. Whose voice was that?

"What's next? I mean, is she going to wake up? Please tell me she's going to wake up."

It was Gabby's voice; I knew it had to be Gabby's voice. Gabby! Gabby! I wanted to scream, but I couldn't see her in the darkness. Someone turn on the lights, I need to see my baby girl.

I began running again, through the pitch black, eerie night. I was lost, unsure of where to find her, confused which direction her voice was coming from. The blackness turned into a forest; I was up on top of a cliff: scared, alone. Light pierced through the sky, lighting up my hands. The freckles and saggy skin that took years of living to consume my body, pushing my veins to the surface, causing pain and aches in places I never realized existed turned to soft, thirty-year-old skin in front of my eyes.

The sun rose in the sky, shining on me more and more with each passing second. My skin glowed in all the places the sun touched, erasing the miles I put on and showing my youth. The prime time in my life. My happiest days.

I saw a shadow in the distance, heard it calling my name and telling me to come home. I touched the pink butterflies that circled my head. I placed my hand out and stared at its sparkling beauty. Did it just smile at me? I felt my heart slowing down as peace filled my heart and soul, my toes tingling.

And then I heard the angel's voice.

"Mom, please don't leave me, please don't go. I'm not ready yet. I need to see you, need to say goodbye. Please open your eyes."

Gabby? I turned around, ran toward her voice through the trees and past the cliff. Gabby, where are you? Gabby! I screamed, panic in my voice. I stopped, looked down at my hands as they once again looked like a fifty-one-year-old's hands, arms and legs, but I didn't care. I wanted to see Gabby, I'd do anything. The lights turned off. Darkness. My eyelids were heavy, I fought the pain to open them, to see her again. I struggled to open my eyes; it was blurry but I could see the image of two people, maybe three at my bedside. I blinked twice, tried again.

"Mom. Mom, you're awake."

Stabbing pain shot up my spine and neck as I focused on turning my head to see her. I fought for this moment and I finally found her. My tongue felt like pine needles against my lips as I stumbled to open them. They were sticking together; I needed to lick them, but I couldn't. I couldn't get my tongue to move the way I wanted it to, needed it to.

I saw a hand from the other side of the bed reach around me and place my glasses on my nose. I wanted to adjust them, but my hands wouldn't move. Once I saw the queen of diamonds, I remembered where I was and I felt something squeezing my lungs. I gasped for air, closed my eyes. Was somebody standing on me?

"It's okay, mom, I'm here. I'm here."

I could hear her sobbing, struggling for air just like me. Something was in my hand. It was soft; I felt pressure. I moved my fingers, squeezed back with all my might, struggled again to open my eyes.

"I love you Mom, I love you. Your biopsy is over. You have your wish for us to know what's wrong with you. Although I didn't like what you did, I mean, I understand, Mom. I know you did it because we will never know what the cause of Grandma's death was. It was just so hard to watch you go through an unnecessary procedure. The doctor said it is Glioblastoma multiforme. Mom, it is the worst kind of cancer there is. It is in your brainstem and..." She stopped talking to compose herself. Her crying was impeding her words and I squeezed her hand once again, even though it hurt to move.

"There is nothing they can do, Mom. I'm praying for a miracle, we all are."

I suddenly realized the other people in the room left. It was just me and Gabby. When did she grow up and turn into this beautiful woman? Where did time go? I closed my eyes and saw her as that five-year-old girl. Pigtails, pink dresses and more energy than anyone I knew. Her strong spirit and love for life was definitely passed down from her father. I opened my eyes again, struggling not to be taken away from her again. Although I felt rested and at peace when I closed my eyes, when I opened them, I felt my heart full of joy and life.

"The hospice nurse said we can bring you home tomorrow. You can finally come home. I'm so sorry you have to go through this. Remember, we are all by your side and love you so much. Fight, Mom, please fight for a few more days with us. I'm just not ready to let you go, not yet," she cried, rubbing my arm.

She leaned down and kissed me on the lips. Her cool lips felt refreshing. They were cracking and filled with fire. She reached into her pocket and dotted her ChapStick on my lips. Although I could no longer rub them together, it felt soothing.

"Mom, I hate to see you in pain like this. Maybe you feel less pain or maybe the drugs took care of that, I dunno. Irene will be here in a couple minutes with Phillip. She took her first steps yesterday, in the hospital here. It was a miracle, I will never forget it. She walked three steps from the chair to the side of your bed. It was almost as if she was walking right to you."

I felt a presence enter the room and then a giggle from a

toddler. I smiled to myself. No one could see it, but I think Gabby knew. Phillip dangled the baby girl a foot or so from my face. I saw her smile, laugh, reach for my long brown curls, which I'm sure were now turning gray without the luxury of boxed hair dye. I wanted to reach out, touch her, hold her in my arms.

Instead, I heard the voice of the nurse behind them. "Time to get you ready for bed, Destiny."

Seriously?

"Mom, we will be back tomorrow to bring you home. I love you," she said, leaning over the side of the bed to kiss me on the forehead.

I let my eyes close and I chased him through the garden, laughing as the butterfly landed on my shoulder.

CHAPTER 13

JANUARY 1997

*G*abby and I arrived at the hospital around nine the next morning. I really had slept little the night before, waiting for a phone call from Judy that never came. My heels tapped the floor, echoing through the bare hallway. The sound of my heels was calming me down, releasing my anxiety and fear.

As we turned the corner, Gabby cried out, "Grammy!" and ran as fast as she could into Judy's arms.

"Hey, baby girl, how are you?"

"Really good. Mommy let me eat cake for breakfast." She leaned in to Judy's ear. "Mom never lets me eat cake for breakfast. I think she misses Daddy."

My entire body went limp as I watched her skip down the hallway, hand in hand with Judy. Judy turned around and grinned at me. I shrugged my shoulders and raised my eyebrows in response, closely following behind them.

"Okay, Gabby, Daddy is right in there. Why don't you go say hello with Grandpa while I talk to your mommy, okay?" she asked, bending down to Gabby's height.

"Okay, Grammy." She took Carl's hand and walked into the room with him.

Judy turned to me. "I'm sorry I didn't call you, but I knew you needed your rest and I didn't want to bother you. Bryan is doing very well. They said his swelling is very minimal and has gotten no worse. They want to monitor him one more night and then he can go home if there are no more changes. Isn't that great?"

"Wow, that's amazing. I can't believe he's doing so well. I was so worried about him."

"He doesn't remember the accident at all, and sometimes he seems to stare off a little, but he's really doing well. You know how strong he is; I'm not surprised."

I could hear a woman's voice in the room.

"Who is in there?" I asked.

"Probably just the nurse, dear," she said, walking into the room and I followed.

The blonde nurse was sitting next to Bryan's bed with Gabby in her lap, playing with her hair. I was in shock.

Bran's head peeked up when he saw me walk in.

"Hey, Dez, you remember Olivia, right?"

I felt my blood pressure rising; I wanted to hide, disappear into thin air. What the hell is she doing here?

"No, I don't believe I do," I replied with a forced smile.

"You know, Olivia Johnson, from high school," he said, confused.

"Oh, yeah, Olivia Johnson, how are you?" I asked, stepping forward. I couldn't take my eyes off of Gabby sitting in that woman's lap.

"I'm doing well. I heard you and Bryan got married, huh? Congratulations. What a beautiful girl you have."

I wondered what it would feel like to mess up that perfect face. Her blonde hair was silky and perfect, pulled back into a ponytail. The prom picture of her and Bryan, crowned king and queen their senior year, flashed into my head. My hands turned into fists, I hid them behind my back.

"Olivia, you haven't changed at all, you look beautiful," Judy spoke, a little too excited as she walked toward her, giving her a welcoming hug that made my skin crawl.

"Oh please, you are making me blush. You are the one that hasn't changed at all, Judy. What is your secret? Please tell."

Her smile was too big, too fake. Did anyone buy this? I looked at Judy, then at Carl. Huge grins lit up their faces with her flattery.

"Olivia here was just telling us she works down the hall in Peds," Carl explained.

"Yeah, I walked down here to talk to the nurses, when I saw Bryan here in ICU. I am so glad you are okay, you must have been so scared with the accident and all."

"I remember nothing. It's all a blur," he replied, staring down at his hands.

"I can only imagine. Well, you sure look amazing after such a traumatizing accident. I'm so glad you are okay. We should really catch up soon. I better get going, I'll come back and check on you later. Oh, and Bryan, if these nurses aren't good to you, just let me know and I'll deal with them. It was so nice seeing you all. And you, Gabby, right?"

Gabby smiled, "Yep."

"You are such a beautiful girl. I hope I get to see you later. Thank you for sitting with me," she said, getting up. Gabby slid off her lap and jumped onto the bed with Bryan.

"I love your hair, Olivia. You are very beautiful," Gabby blushed, smiling.

"No, I love your hair. You are the most beautiful little girl

I have ever seen. How would you like it if I come back in a bit and took you to get some hot cocoa with me? I mean, if it is okay with your mom and dad."

Gabby jumped off the bed and came running to me. "Please Mommy, please can I go with Olivia? Please."

I stared at her for a moment. I didn't want her going with Bryan's beautiful high school girlfriend, but I didn't want to look like the bad guy either.

"We do have the best hot chocolate in Duluth, I promise," Olivia said, trying to persuade me by tricking her way into Gabby's heart. What a bitch to use a sweet little five-year-old to impress Bryan. I really hoped he wasn't buying any of this act.

"We aren't staying real long, but if we're here, that's fine."

"Bye," they all called out after her.

"What a sweet girl. What ever happened with the two of you?" Judy asked as if his wife wasn't in the room.

"We just went our separate ways, I guess."

"Gabby, would you like me to take you to the gift shop so your mom and dad can have some time together?" Judy asked.

"Can I Mom, can I?"

"Yes, just don't ask your grandma for too much."

She kissed me on the cheek before running out in the hall, Carl and Judy closely behind her.

I turned to Bryan.

"How are you feeling?"

"I'm doing much better today. I still have a headache, but the pain isn't as bad. Did you really not recognize Olivia?"

"Not until you said her last name," I lied, unable to look him in the eye. "What happened between the two of you? I know she moved away, but you never told me why the two of you broke up."

"I really don't know."

"You don't know?" I asked, rolling my eyes.

"No, I really don't. She left right after graduation. I mean, technically she never even broke up with me. She didn't say where she was going or why she was leaving. It's always kept me wondering. I admit, I really want to find out. Obviously I don't still have feelings for her or anything, I just am curious why she would leave without even saying goodbye. I have always wondered if it was something I did."

"Hmm, well I guess you will get your chance."

We sat there in awkward silence for a few minutes until Bryan finally broke the ice.

"So, I get to go home tomorrow."

"Yeah, that's what I heard. Are you coming home with us? I mean, where do we stand, Bryan?"

"Well, I already asked my parents if I could stay with them for a little while. You know until I find a place of my own."

He looked up at me nervously, and I forced myself not to flip out at him.

"Okay," I mumbled.

Fight for him, Destiny, fight hard. "Well, if you ever change your mind, I would really love to start over with you. I love you, Bryan."

"I love you too, but I just can't right now. I don't think it is good for any of us. I can never trust you again after what you did. I worry if we got back together I would never get it out of my head. This is for the best. I know it will be hard at first, but you will be okay and so will Gabby. Living in a house with parents that fight all the time isn't good for any kid."

I was focusing hard on not crying. He couldn't see me like this. I needed to fight for him, for us.

"Also, I was wondering if Gabby could come stay at my mom's with me. I have another week off of work, doctor's orders, and I would like to spend it with her. What do you think? You are still working at Johnson Law Office, right?" He sat up a little taller, studying me.

"She can stay with you for a couple days, but I want to be with her too. We can work something out. As for the law office, no way would I continue working with Casey after what he did." I felt my fear turn into anger, panic at the thought of Bryan and Olivia together. I shook it out of my head.

"Because he told me?" he snapped.

"No, not because he told you. Because he told me I had to leave you, that you were too good for me. He only told you because I quit. I told him I wouldn't keep it from you any longer, I couldn't. Bryan you have to believe me, I don't know how this happened. I don't know how I ended up in bed with him. I remember nothing from that night; I would never do that to you," I cried out.

"Dez, you don't need to apologize or make up lies. What's done is done. We're over."

I heard a knock on the open door behind me. I turned around to see the devil standing right there behind me.

"Is this a bad time? I can come back," Olivia smiled. Way too big.

Those perfect teeth, hot pink scrubs, who did she think she was kidding. She would take Bryan from me, I could feel it.

CHAPTER 14

*G*abby and I were both exhausted when we finally made it back to Hibbing, after the long emotional day. My eyelids were heavy and my headache, severe. Bryan would come home tomorrow morning. I was just glad he wouldn't be at the hospital with Olivia anymore.

I opened my front door without even a thought of taking out my dry contacts or even brushing my teeth. I put Gabby to bed and went upstairs to my bedroom, stripping down to a t-shirt and underwear, before turning off the light and slipping under the covers. I had no strength left. I wanted to sleep the days away; I had no fight left in me. I felt dark, lonely, and rejected. I closed my eyes and prayed for a better day tomorrow.

A LOUD NOISE STARTLED ME. I glanced at my alarm clock; it was one thirty-two in the morning. Wide awake, I was sick from the reality of the last twenty-four hours. Anxiety took over my chest, leaving it burning, and sped up my breathing as I tried to figure out what the noise was. I listened for a moment and thought maybe I was just dreaming it. I took a deep breath, rolled over, and closed my eyes to fall back asleep. They shot open again in the darkness; was that my door creaking open? I was scared to turn my head, my anxiety leaving me paralyzed.

I was struggling just to breathe. The intruder couldn't know I was awake. The soft footsteps became louder as someone neared the side of my bed. I'm not ready to die. I thought about what weapons I had within reach. The only thing I had by my bed was a nightstand with books and my phone. I had no time to dial 9-1-1. I thought about kneeing the intruder in the groin, clawing their face so that the DNA would be under my nails when my body was found. If my body was found.

Could it be Gabby? No way Gabby would knock and call out for me. Was someone here to rob me? Kill me? I couldn't be sure. My body locked up as I felt the pressure of some-one's weight on the bed. I could hear breathing, heavy like a smoker. My eyes adjusted to the darkness and I could see a shadow lingering on the wall.

It moved forward, I could feel a nose in my hair, smelling me? I was as still as possible, not moving an inch or letting them know I was awake until I figured out who it was. Why were they here? It all happened so fast. He jumped on top of me, straddling me between his legs and held my wrists down into my bed, hard. I couldn't move.

"Please stop!" I screamed. "Who are you? What are you doing here?"

His face was inches from mine. The foul smell of whisky burned my nostrils and turned my stomach. He giggled, intensifying my heart rate.

"Casey! Casey get off me! Now!" I screamed.

I thought about Gabby and prayed we wouldn't wake her. I was scared he would hurt me, hurt her.

"Oh Destiny, why do you have to be running your mouth?"

"What are you talking about? I'm not running my mouth, I've been in the hospital all day."

He squeezed my wrists harder, pinning me tighter. "You don't think I know? Why did you tell Bryan about our talk?" He clenched his teeth, spitting on my face when he talked.

"I didn't, I didn't. What talk? Casey, you need to get out now. I won't call the cops, I promise. Please, just leave!" My voice came out angry, scared.

"I'm not going anywhere. Why do you have to be like this? I told you to leave him, but you couldn't do that now, could you? You couldn't do this the easy way, you had to be a stupid lying bitch." He moved his face, so it was just inches from mine. His breath made me cringe as I turned my face away from him.

"You are the one that told Bryan about us, this is not on me. You called him right after I left your office. You were the one that betrayed and lied to me."

"You should have left him when I told you to. Now you get to watch her steal your man and there is nothing you can do. You have no chance, none. She will ruin you, ruin you," he said, loosening his grip on my arms.

"Who is she? What are you talking about, Casey?"

"I'm finally free. If you even try to get back with Bryan, I will find you and I will finish what I just started. You will never be safe." He grabbed my cheeks, squeezing them together beneath his big, strong, sweaty hands.

"Free from what? What are you talking about?"

He got off the bed and headed toward the door, ignoring my questions. He turned around to look at me.

"Oh, and if you call the police, I will kill you. This isn't a threat. It's a promise."

And then he was gone.

I laid in bed crying, unable to move. Then Gabby's face came into my head. I didn't even put pants on as I leaped my way down the stairs, my legs moving faster than they'd ever moved before. Her door swung open, and she was fast asleep. Making my way to the front window, I stopped to listen, but I could hear only the sound of my rapid heart. No one in sight. I opened up the front door, noticing it was unlocked.

Did I lock the door when we came in? I was so tired, I couldn't be sure. I saw his boot prints in the snow that led to tire tracks. He was gone. I sighed, relieved it was over and he was finally gone. I turned around and headed back inside, noticing the goosebumps on my arms. I could not feel the bitter cold of the Minnesota winter, because the fear kept me warm and wide awake. I locked the front door and turned the deadbolt, making my way to the kitchen.

"How did he know I talked to Bryan? Was Bryan still talking to him? He had to be," I whispered to myself. I laid down on the couch, afraid to go back to my room, just in case. No way was I taking a chance and calling the police. Maybe I didn't know Bryan at all. Casey had definitely changed a lot since his father died. Why was he so set on ruining my relationship with Bryan, anyway? And who would steal him from me? None of it made any sense.

CHAPTER 15

"*W*hy isn't Daddy coming home?"

I got down on my knees and put my hands on both of her shoulders. "Honey, Daddy will stay with Grammy and Gramps for a couple days and he really wants you there with him. Mommy has a bunch of stuff to do around here and then you can come home and see me."

"But won't Daddy be coming home too? Why isn't he coming home, Mommy?"

I wasn't ready for this; I had no answers for her.

"Well, Gabby, I'm just not sure yet. It will be fun. You can hang out with everyone, have some alone time with Daddy, it will be a blast. Did you pack your favorite teddy bear and blanky in your backpack? I have all your clothes in the suitcase."

"Yeah," she said, hanging her head.

"It will be okay. Mommy will be right here. You got to go help take care of Daddy, okay."

"Okay, Mom."

Gabby just stared out the window on the way to Judy and

Carl's. Her young innocence kept her from seeing what was really going on, and for now, I was okay with that.

As we walked in the door to their house, she saw her daddy and her eyes lit up as she jumped in his arms. He looked a little dizzy, but played it off.

"Honey, you need to be careful with Daddy. Remember, he hit his head hard and needs you to help him get better. Why don't you read him a book?" Judy suggested.

"Give Mommy a hug," I said, trying to catch her before she took off.

"I love you, Mommy."

"I love you too, baby." I couldn't hide the tears in my eyes as I watched her run away with excitement.

She stopped quickly and turned around.

"I'm sorry, Daddy, I'll wait for you. I forget I need to take care of you."

I smiled and closed the door behind me.

I MADE myself a salad and began folding the clothes I pulled out from the dryer. Walking into Gabby's room, I noticed her favorite blue blanky on her bed. The one she promised me she packed.

"Gabby," I said aloud, shaking my head and rolling my eyes as I picked it up.

Dressed in my running clothes, I put blue blanky in a small backpack and grabbed my headphones off the microwave. Three miles sounded like the perfect distance for a run today. Walking outside, I took a deep breath of Minnesota air. The snowflakes were collecting on my face and tickling my nose. I started off with a slow jog and quickly picked up my pace. I needed to get Bryan to listen, to understand that I didn't mean to hurt him. That I never felt that way about Casey. Why did I do this to him? These thoughts circled in my head for years. Sometimes I really believed I could move past it all, but in the back of my mind, none of it made sense.

I wasn't attracted to him like that. How could I not remember? I needed some time with Bryan, needed to make him fall back in love with me. No more secrets.

With my in-law's house in view, my jog turned to a walk. A red car was parked in their driveway, unfamiliar to me. I saw her long blonde hair and red hat, talking to Bryan. Stopping, I blinked my eyes and stared at her as they stood next to the garage, smiling, laughing. I put my hands on my thighs, unaware of the heavy breathing and weakness in my knees. Their heads got closer, their lips were pressed together. That's when I began running. It felt like I was running in slow motion, taking forever to get to them. She turned around in surprise. I heard a scream and then I was on top of her, punching her and pulling her hair. My arms felt heavy, but I didn't care. I wanted to mess up that pretty little face.

Suddenly, I was being dragged away, and it was all over. Bryan was screaming at me, yelling for Olivia to go. Then someone turned off the lights and all I could see and feel was darkness.

THE PAIN in my knuckles woke me up. I looked around, unsure of what happened. I felt the touch of fingers in my hair. I was on his lap, on my couch. Exhaustion and comfort ran through my veins as I lifted my head and turned my body over.

"Bryan?"

"Good morning Mike Tyson," he laughed.

"What happened? How did I get here? I had the

strangest…" Oh no, that really happened, I realized, looking at my swollen hands.

"Dream? It wasn't a dream," he laughed again. "I have never seen you like that, fighting so hard for me. It shocked me."

He didn't seem like he hated me. That was good.

"Olivia should have never kissed me like that. I don't blame you for what you did. It was way too soon. I mean, we were talking, and I was laughing and then, well, she kissed me and then was tackled to the ground."

I laughed. "I dunno what got into me. I'm so sorry."

"Listen, this changes nothing. If Gabby would have seen, I mean, that could have been terrible."

"I know I'm so sorry."

"Well, that too, but I mean Olivia kissing me right there. I did not know she would do that, and I'm so sorry you had to see that."

"Is she okay?" I asked, unsure of whether I really cared.

"I don't know, I kinda kicked her out before I could even see her face. I hope so. Destiny, please tell me what happened that night between you and Casey. I'm ready to listen."

I took a deep breath. None of it made much sense to me, so how would Bryan understand or believe me?

"Well, I will tell you what I remember. You were working afternoons, and I was with Chloe rock climbing in Duluth. When I got home, Casey came over upset because his dad died. Looking for you. He poured us both a drink and then I had a shot of Tequila Rose and that's it. The next thing I knew, I woke up in bed with him, naked."

"One shot and you don't remember? I just can't take your word on this one, Dez. You must have had more to drink than that."

I shook my head, sitting up. "I know it makes little sense, Bryan, but you have to believe me. I never saw Casey like that. Then, after I left the hospital and drove home, Casey broke into our bedroom in the middle of the night. I mean, I'm sure I left the door open, but he snuck into our room."

Bryan stood up, his eyes wide with fury. "He what!"

"Calm down, please. Let me tell you what happened."

Bryan put his hands on his hips and just stared at me, becoming impatient.

"He snuck into our room and threatened me, saying something about how I should have left you when he told me to and—"

"When he told you to?"

"Oh, yeah. Well, when I was at the law office, he told me I had to leave you or he would tell you what I did. I went home to tell you, but he had already told you by the time I got there."

"And I told him I never wanted to speak to him again," Bryan yelled.

"You did? Okay, then why did he tell me when he broke into our bedroom I needed to quit running my mouth and something about how she will take you away from me and there is nothing I can do?" I asked, trying to figure out what Casey was talking about.

"I didn't talk to anyone. You saw everyone I talked to. That makes little sense. Who is she?" he asked, confused.

"Oh my god," I said, jumping to my feet. "Olivia."

"Olivia?"

"Yeah, he must be talking to Olivia. I mean, it makes sense unless someone else has tried to kiss you since you got home."

"No, Olivia would never do that. I don't know if I believe any of this," he said, turning his back to me.

"Bryan, please trust me," I pleaded.

"How can I trust you after all of this? You slept with my

best friend, my best friend, Dez!" He put his palm on his forehead.

"I am still the same person you married. I am still me, Bryan."

"I just don't think Liv would do that. I mean, I wouldn't put it past Bryan, but Liv?"

He looked defeated, confused, unsure of what to believe. It hurt as I realized he still had feelings for her. I could see it in his face. He was feeling guilty.

"Did he also lie about you standing outside the bathroom door in your lingerie when he walked out?"

I felt the color draining out of my face. "Yes, it's true, but I thought it was you. I was trying to surprise you, you have to believe me."

"Really? With Casey at the house? Seems hard to believe," he said, challenging me.

"No, the lights were off and you were sleeping in the basement. I really thought he was gone, Bryan. I never had an interest in him, never will."

"I actually believe you." He paused before finally continuing, "But you still pulled away from me for five years and couldn't tell me you cheated on me. I feel terrible that he did that to you and I'd love to beat the crap out of him, but how could you not be honest with me? I thought we were a team, I just don't know if I could ever trust you again."

"I hope one day you can forgive me."

He rolled his eyes and walked away.

CHAPTER 16

"I have to get to the bottom of this," I told Jill, before deciding to take off to Duluth to knock at Olivia's door.

I was done playing games with her. I needed to talk to her face to face, although I realized she may just shut the door on me before we got to talk at all. I knew that was a risk I would have to take. I really didn't mind apologizing for what I did, it was childish. Even though this bitch was trying to steal my husband from me, he really wasn't mine to lose anymore. The thought of him with her made my headache return. I turned up the volume on the radio and got lost in the songs, not wanting to think about it anymore.

Once in Duluth, I turned right onto Haines Road as I made my way down the large hill in Duluth. Although the site of Lake Superior was quite a view, I really wasn't in the mood for sightseeing. I watched the signs as I made my way to Grand Avenue, stopping to take a right on Forty-Fourth Street West. I made my way slowly down the street until I saw the small bright green house with the numbers nailed to the side of the house.

Was I making the right decision? It was stupid of me to think I could just show up at her house and she'd be here. I couldn't see her red vehicle parked out front, but it could be in the back. I got out of the car and made my way up the wobbly wooden porch. Every step I took, I wondered if the stairs would break. The red paint was chipping off and the green siding missing pieces all over. It was a dump. I rang the doorbell and held my breath.

I could hear a dog barking and a boy yelling, "Be right there!"

A small head appeared in the window and he smiled at the sight of me.

"Hi," he said, opening the door. "May I help you?"

He had to be around thirteen or fourteen. I must have gotten the wrong house.

"I'm sorry, I must be at the wrong house. Do you know where Olivia lives?"

"Ma'am, you have the right house. Olivia lives here."

It shocked me, "Oh, okay. My name is Destiny. I didn't know Olivia had a—"

Casey's voice cut me off, "Travis, why don't you go upstairs and play. It's for me."

"Okay, Dad."

Dad? Did I just hear him right? Did he just call Casey Dad? What was going on here? That couldn't be right. I was so confused.

"Dad?" I asked, scrunching my eyes together in disbelief.

I backed up as he walked onto the porch, shutting the door behind him.

"Destiny, what are you doing here?" He was angry, hostile.

"Well, I came here to see Olivia and I am completely shocked to see you here. What the hell is going on, Dad?"

"You shouldn't have come here," he said, looking over his shoulder and behind me.

"I'm not leaving until you tell me what is going on. How can you be that child's father? What is he talking about?"

He shook his head and stepped closer to me.

"Listen, I will tell you everything, you just need to get out of here, fast. If Olivia finds out you were here. If Olivia finds out you know about Travis, I could lose everything that matters to me. Listen, there is so much you don't know. If you want me to tell you everything, you need to go home. I can meet you at McDonald's at noon tomorrow if you promise not to tell anyone anything, especially Bryan. Please, Dez. It will all make sense tomorrow, I promise."

I was in shock. I couldn't believe what I was hearing. I had so many questions.

"No, Casey, I need to know now! I demand answers! I don't care if Olivia sees us talking. What the hell is going on here?"

"I swear to god... you know what? I have done some terrible things to you and I know that it is hard for you to trust me right now, but you have to believe me. There is so much you need to know. Can you please just meet me tomorrow?" he asked, inching me down the stairs toward my car.

"I don't know what you are up to Casey, but you better have one hell of an explanation. I don't know why I am giving you the benefit of the doubt right now, but you seem terrified about something. I don't think I have ever seen you scared before, so I will listen to you. You better tell me the truth tomorrow and I mean it," I warned him, putting my finger in his face.

"Thank you so much, now please go," he rushed me, opening up my car door for me.

"You owe me," I warned as I pulled away.

My impatience had me second guessing why I let him push me away. Why I left without answers. He just looked so scared, so paranoid. Casey a dad? Olivia the mom? Travis had to be about thirteen, possibly fourteen. Why would Casey hide this from Bryan? Why didn't he want him to know? A child seemed like something you would want to tell your best friend. Was he scared Bryan would be mad he hooked up with his ex-girlfriend? I didn't even know he knew Olivia lived in Duluth. The questions were killing me. I knew I had no choice than to wait until I met with Casey tomorrow, but it was so hard to wait so long without telling anyone.

"JILL, you will not believe what just happened!" I yelled, coming into her house, looking for her.

"Don't tell me you went to see Olivia," she said, meeting me in the kitchen.

"I did, and you won't believe who answered the door."

"Who? You're killing me here."

"Casey!" I screamed.

"Casey? As in Bryan's friend, Casey?"

"Yeah, well, he didn't actually answer the door, their kid did."

"Their kid? How is that possible? How old was their kid?" She seemed just as blown away with this information as I did.

"His name is Travis, and he was about thirteen, maybe fourteen years old. I don't know, but Casey was pissed, and he told the kid to go upstairs. And do you know what the kid said to him?"

"What?"

"He said, okay Dad. Can you believe it? Okay, Dad," I explained, my voice getting more excited as I talked.

"You have got to be kidding me. So, Olivia and Casey had

a kid? That is just absolutely crazy. What did Casey say about all of this? He had to be hiding it for a reason."

"Well, he seemed to be very troubled that I was there and paranoid that she would come home. So, he told me he would explain everything tomorrow if I met him at McDonald's at noon. Does that seem weird to you?"

"It sounds like she is pretty evil. McDonald's here or in Duluth?"

I thought for a moment, "He really wasn't specific, I mean I think he meant here. There are so many McDonald's in Duluth. I would think if he meant there, he would have specified which McDonald's, right?"

"Yes, I wouldn't worry too much about it. Sounds like you were both nervous. I just can't believe you left without making him tell you more."

"Oh, I tried, Jill. There was no way he would tell me anything there."

"Bryan will be so pissed. Are you going to go tell him? Call him?"

I stepped closer to her. "No, Jill. Promise me you won't tell Bryan until I talk to Casey tomorrow—"

I was cut off to the loud ringing of her home phone on the wall.

"Hang on," she said, looking at the Caller ID. "It's Mom, I have to get this. Hey Mom," she said, picking up the phone. "Mom, slow down! I can't understand you. Who? Who's Andrew?"

Her eyes opened up wide as she dropped the phone which was caught just before hitting the ground by the short cord and bounced back up and down a few times like a bungee cord.

"Jill? Is everything okay? Is Mom okay?" I asked, diving for the phone and picking it up.

"Mom—"

"Mom, are you there?" I asked, even though I could hear her screaming something into the phone. I looked up at Jill, confused.

"It's your dad, he found me! What do I do?"

CHAPTER 17

"*D*ad called? Are you sure?"

"Yes Destiny, I'm sure. He said he was coming to town and when I told him to stay away," she broke out into sobs and could no longer continue talking.

I could tell she was drunk.

"Mom, stay right there, Jill and I are on our way. Don't go anywhere!" I yelled before hanging up.

I grabbed my keys off of the counter and began running to the door. When I saw Jill wasn't following me, I turned around and ran back to get her.

"Jill, lets go! Mom's in trouble, I'll drive."

"I can't."

"Jill," I said, pulling on her arm, "we need to go now."

"I can't Destiny, I just can't."

I could tell she was obviously quite worried about seeing him again. I just needed to get Mom out of that house, fast.

"Okay, I understand. I'll be right back, okay?" I said, giving her a quick hug. "It will be okay, don't worry. I'll be right back."

When she nodded, I dashed out of the house to get to Mom before he did.

WE GOT BACK to Jill's before Mom could say anything. She just cried the whole way. I tried to pry the Busch Light out of her hand, but it would only cause a mess. Beer in one hand, twelve pack in the other, typical mom.

Jill got up and hugged her.

"He found me, Jill, he found me."

"Mom, it will be okay. Did you call the cops?"

"They said since I dun have a restraining order or evidence, there is nothing they can do," she drunkenly slurred sobbing, then guzzled the rest of her beer.

"Mom, you need to sober up so we can talk about this," I told her.

"I am sober! I like my beer, Dez. If you came to see me once in a while with Gabby, you would know that, but you dun know anything bout me. You says I'm a drunk, but you dunno my life or what I bin through. Back off," she said, pushing me away. "I'm not an alcoholic, I like me beer."

I groaned in Jill's direction.

"I heard that," she said, laying down on Jill's white sofa.

I couldn't believe Jill was just going to let her sleep on her brand new couch, but we both knew Mom would scream at us and probably storm out if one of us said anything to her. She could take no criticism and was non-confrontational. She'd never talk about it again, then the next time we would come over she would pretend it never happened. Maybe she was sometimes too drunk to remember the next day, who knows.

I could hear her snoring. Walking toward her, I bent down to take the beer out of her hand so it wouldn't spill while she was sleeping.

"What are we going to do?" Jill asked.

I walked over to Mom's purse and pulled the strap off her arm. I carried her purse to the table and dumped it out.

"What are you doing, Dez? What if she wakes up?" Jill asked, obviously apprehensive.

"It's okay, Jill. I just want to make sure her inhaler is in here in case she has an asthma attack."

"Oh, okay."

As I dumped the contents of the smaller pockets in her big purse out, two bottles of pills came rolling out, along with the inhaler. One bottle was OxyContin, and the other was Xanax. I knew Xanax was for her anxiety, but why was she taking Oxys?

"Jill, why was mom taking OxyContin?"

"I wasn't supposed to tell you, but she said her back has been hurting her. She was afraid you would judge her."

"She was afraid I would judge her?"

"She's been taking them every day, she told me it really helps."

I examined the bottles closer. I dug in her purse and I could feel another bottle of some sort. I found another hidden pocket and two empty bottles of OxyContin were in there.

"Well, all three bottles have different doctor's names on them. This one says her primary doctor, Dr. Hanson, this one says Dr. Joneson, and the third bottle says Dr. Brinley," I said, pointing at their names.

"What do you think that means? Do you think she is going to different doctors because she is addicted to Opioids?"

"Yes, that's exactly what I'm thinking. That or she's selling them."

"Oh my god, Dez, I just don't think I can take any more

bad news tonight. There has to be another explanation for this."

"What other explanation can she have? And OxyContin can give you anxiety, which explains the Xanax."

"Yeah, but Mom has anxiety already. I just don't want to deal with this right now. Can we put them back, please?" she asked, worried.

"I need to count them first, though, just to make sure she isn't taking too many."

"Fine."

I counted twenty-nine and wrote it on my hand so I wouldn't forget. I would just have to count them again some-time tomorrow. I packed up her purse and left it, along with her inhaler, on the table in front of the couch.

Jill and I walked into the kitchen.

"Do you really think Dad will hurt her?" I asked.

She grabbed a pizza out of the freezer and preheated the oven. "Yeah, he's violent. Mom never filed any charges against him all those years, so he has no criminal record for domestics."

"You would think he would have done this to someone else in the past. It isn't like suddenly he could be this abusive man.

"Unless they were all scared like Mom."

"I guess," I said, pulling up a stool at her breakfast bar.

"You don't remember how bad he was, do you?"

"No, not really. I was a baby."

"Destiny, Mom would scream all the time. One time I came downstairs, and she told me he beat her with a frying pan. I wasn't much older than Gabby."

"Are you serious? A frying pan?" I asked in disbelief.

"Yes, he's crazy, I told you. One time he pushed me down the stairs, Destiny. One time he even broke her nose."

"You have to be kidding me. I can't believe she started

drinking after she left him. I mean, just knowing that drugs and alcohol is what caused him to be the way he is."

"I really don't know. I guess she is just trying to numb the pain. Why do you think she was so hard on you when you were depressed, after you left Bryan and you were staying with her?"

"I don't know, I guess I just thought she was just being Mom."

"No, she is very depressed and has been for a very long time," she explained, removed the pizza from the cardboard and putting it in the oven.

"You are putting that in before it's preheated?"

"I like it better that way."

"Well, alcohol will only make her more depressed. Jill, she doesn't even think she has a problem."

"Yeah, only because everyone is scared to tell her she does. I mean, could you imagine Mom at an intervention? She would literally be so angry she would just walk out of there and never talk to any of us again. She would probably get even more depressed. The only friends she has left are the two ladies she works with."

"Yeah, well, I just don't know how to help her anymore."

She walked toward me, placing her hands on my shoulders while I sat on the stool.

"Dez, she can't get help until she realizes she has a problem. All we can do is just take her keys when she wants to drive and keep our distance."

"It's easier said than done."

"Oh, trust me, I know. Right now we just need to focus on keeping her safe from Dad."

"Well, I'm glad she doesn't have a gun."

CHAPTER 18

Sitting at McDonald's, I took a sip of my hot coffee while watching kids play in the play-place. The moms ate their meals in peace while their kids made new friends and played hard, their only worries that entangled their minds was when their mom would make them go home.

I saw Casey through the enormous windows, walking into McDonald's and coming to find me immediately. He looked just as disturbed as yesterday, if not worse. His eyes sunk in, as if he hadn't slept all night, and he kept looking over his shoulder. He sat across from me at the table.

"Do you ever notice how content children are? How it doesn't take much to please them?"

"Okay, what are you talking about?" he asked, sounding annoyed.

"Nothing. Start talking."

"You know back in high school when Liv and Bryan were dating?"

"Yeah, get to the point," I responded, impatient.

"Liv and I were close, very close friends," he said, emphasizing the word friends. "One night she came over, very upset about a fight she had with Bryan. She entrusted in me that she wanted to make love to Bryan, but Bryan wanted to wait until marriage."

"Until marriage? I didn't know that."

"You didn't know you were his first?"

"No. I don't think I was."

"Really, then who was?"

I sat there for a moment, thinking about who he told me he slept with. "I guess I just always thought he slept with Olivia."

Was he really a virgin when he slept with me? If so, how did I not know?

"Anyway, like I said, she came over upset. She was vulnerable, I was horny. One thing led to another and... you know."

He nodded his head at me. I rolled my eyes back.

"Okay, continue the story."

"She never told me she was pregnant until right before you and I slept together."

Hearing him say we slept together made me want to vomit.

"Wait a minute, she didn't tell you she was pregnant?"

"No, right after they diagnosed my dad with Leukemia, she called me and told me I had to break the two of you up and told me we had a son."

"Wow, what is that girl's problem with me?"

"It has nothing to do with you. She is totally obsessed with Bryan. Anyway, Travis was nine by the time she told me about him. I told her I would do it after my dad was doing better, then he died. I was so upset after he died, I went to Liv's house and demanded she let me see my son. She told me the only way she would is if I did something for her and I agreed."

"You slept with me," I said under my breath.

"Let me finish. I fell in love with Travis. He meant the world to me. That night, we played video games and colored for hours. The next morning, Liv gave me a roofie and told me I needed to get you alone and slip it in your drink. The two of you were married at the time, so she knew it would take something enormous to break the two of you up."

"You roofied me!" I screamed, getting up and glaring at him.

He stood up shyly, looking around to make sure people weren't staring.

"How could you? How could you?" I repeated, not caring who heard or how loud I was. "Did you rape me? You know it is considered rape if the person you are sleeping with is drugged, right?"

I was sure my face was bright with fury, I could feel the anger pulsating in my veins, my hands now fists at my side.

"Sit down, sit down, Dez. Let me finish, please. I did not rape you, I promise."

"You didn't rape me?"

He was so confusing.

"No, I wouldn't rape you, give me some credit here. I set it up to look like you had sex with me. At first, Liv wanted me to tell Bryan we slept together, but I just couldn't ruin our friendship. I begged her to just let it eat at you. I'm so sorry, Destiny, I just knew it would kill you. I mean, you carrying a secret like sleeping with his best friend would tear the two of you apart. I know there is no way I could ever make it up to you, but I owe you this explanation. I was so selfish."

My anger turned to a loud whisper as I leaned over the table.

"All this time I thought I cheated on my husband and you set me up? You ruined years of my marriage for your own selfish advantage? How could you? What did I do to you to make you think this was okay?"

"Dez, I know, I'm so sorry," he said, his eyes tearing up.

"You're sorry? You're sorry? You made my child have an unhappy home life because you were afraid your son would grow up without you? Ugg, what about the day you threatened me at the office? Casey, you broke into my house and snuck into my bedroom," I said, my voice getting louder.

He put his hand on my arm, and I jerked it away.

"Don't you dare."

"Please let me finish. I know you are angry. It was Liv's idea for me to hire you. At first she wanted me to make you fall in love with me, but I just couldn't. I know it seems like the way I bullied you was horrible, but could you imagine if I would have constantly hit on you?"

"It would have been a lot easier, Casey, I would never be interested in you. You are definitely not my type. I would rather die then look at your pitiful face ever again. What makes you think I could ever think of you that way? You know I love Bryan."

"I tried to scare you away from him, warn you. You were too strong, your love was too strong."

"Why are you telling me all of this? What do you get out of this, Casey?"

"She's horrible to Travis, just horrible. She makes him clean the house, do the laundry, cook dinner."

"So, she's teaching him independence, my mom made me clean too when I was his age."

"No, it's not like that. She is crazy, seriously crazy. She locks herself in her bedroom and only comes out to scream at Travis and tell him everything he's doing wrong. Dez, she hates him because he's my son and not Bryan's. She drinks all the time and sometimes she hits him. He cries all the time, I can't just give up on him right now."

"I'm sorry, Casey, I had no idea. It still doesn't excuse you for what you did to Bryan and me. That poor boy. She really is crazy and now she is trying to win over my husband's heart and there is nothing I can do about it."

He looked nervous.

"What's the catch, Casey? I know there is something you need from me."

"Destiny, do you want him back?"

"I don't need your help," I said through my clenched jaw.

"I know you don't, but I need yours. Did you tell Bryan about what I said yesterday."

"No I didn't, actually. Against my better judgment."

"I know you're angry, just listen. If you can just hold out a little longer. Olivia was so happy I broke the two of you up, she promised me she will sign the paperwork giving me full custody of Travis. She doesn't want Bryan to know about him. She said as long as I move away and never tell Bryan the truth."

"Doesn't she care about her child at all?"

"I told you she's obsessed with Bryan. I promise I will tell Bryan everything, right after she signs the papers. I will literally drop off the paperwork and go tell him immediately."

"Why should I trust you?"

"Because I need to make this right with you and with my best friend, I just don't want Travis in the middle either."

"What's the point? Bryan doesn't love me like that anymore," I said, putting my chin to my chest and covering my eyes with my hands.

"Maybe that's true, but the truth will set you free."

I stood up from the table and put my sunglasses on.

"I'm doing this for Travis and for Bryan. I am not doing this for you, Casey. What you did ruined me. I hope you can no longer sleep at night and from the rings under your eyes, you may just have a conscience after all."

I turned around and walked out the door without another

word. How long was I going to wait before Bryan could finally know the truth? If I saw them kiss one more time, so help me god.

CHAPTER 19

"Well, how did it go?" Jill asked, anxiously waiting by the door when I got there.

"What, did you wait right there the entire time I was gone?"

"No, there is a Home Improvement marathon on. I have been watching it since you left. Then I heard you pull up. So, how did it go?"

I told her about my conversation with Casey, and she seemed to believe his story.

"Well, you are doing the right thing. What's a few more days without telling Bryan? I mean, Casey is a jerk, but it's obvious she doesn't care very much about her kid. It explains why he's been so crazy. I can't believe after all of this, you never even slept with him. I bet it's killing you. Not being able to tell Bryan you didn't cheat on him?"

"Yeah, well, I'm sure it won't change anything. I am worried he is falling for Olivia. Do you think he is?" I said, taking a bottle of water out of her fridge.

"I dunno, but I think he will definitely be relieved. You are doing the right thing here."

"I hope so. Where's Mom?"

Jill patted down her too short pleated skirt.

"She went home right after you left around noon. She wanted to get some sleep, and I told her we would pick her up after you got home."

"Jill! What if Dad shows up?"

"Destiny, you know Mom, she wasn't taking no for an answer, what could I do? You know how stubborn she is when she makes up her mind about something. And she told me I couldn't come with, so I waited for you."

"Thanks a lot," I said, grabbing my jacket and nudging her into the fridge.

"Hey!" she called back, laughing.

MOM HAD three garbages stacked on her front porch. The smell of rotten food made us both hold our breath as we got closer.

"Yuck, Jill. I wonder what the inside of her house looks like," I said as we exchanged glances.

"I'll bring these out to the dumpster and meet you inside."

"You sure you can carry them? Need some help?"

"No, go ahead."

"Mom!" I yelled, opening up her front door. I walked into the kitchen, "Mom?" I made my way up the stairs, beer bottles all over her house. Luckily, our house wasn't this bad growing up. Then again, Jill and I were always cleaning up after her.

Her bedroom door was shut. I knocked as I peeked my head in, "Mom."

I saw three open bottles of pills on her bed and a bottle of whisky tipped over. I grabbed the bottle and shook her. I touched her hand. It was limp and felt cold. I jerked her body on her back. She looked so pale. I felt her face. It was ice cold. My heart began beating rapidly as I shook her harder.

"Mom!" I screamed, blood-curdling scream. "Mom, wake up!" I yelled as loud as I could.

"No. No. No." I heard Jill mutter behind me as she made her way to the bed.

I tried to feel for her pulse, but I could only feel the beat of my own when I touched her. I shook her again.

"Mom, wake up, Mom!" Jill screamed behind me.

"Call nine-one-one Jill, call nine-one-one, now!"

I picked up her limp body and dragged her to the floor. She didn't even seem heavy. I felt for her sternum, placed my two fingers underneath, then adjusted my hands so my fingers were interlocking and began CPR. Thirty compressions to two breaths. I was exhausted by the time the paramedics got there and took over. I had to leave the room as they huddled around her with a gurney. It didn't matter, there was no room for us.

Jill and I stood outside hugging as the paramedics took her away. We both knew she wasn't breathing. We both knew she was gone. We were too late.

"Let's go," Jill said, making her way to my car.

I PICKED up my cell phone and Jill nodded her head in agreement as I dialed Bryan's number in.

"Dez?"

"Hey Bryan, are you with Gabby right now?" I asked, pressing my lips together to stop myself from crying.

"Yeah, we are at the grocery store. We are just checking out. Did you want to talk to her? Gabby, it's your—"

"No!" I screamed, cutting him off.

"Is everything okay?"

"No, Bryan, it's not okay. Can you drop Gabby off at your mom's and meet me at home, please?"

"Yeah… just… just let me pay for these groceries. I'll be there in ten."

"Are you sure you don't want to come in? You really shouldn't be alone right now, Jill."

"I'm sure I just need some time to go home and shower. I have a feeling it will be a rough next couple of days. I will call Aunt Jane and Uncle Chuck to tell them about Mom."

"What about Denise and Kari from her work? Do you want me to call them?" I asked as she shut the door and walked over to the driver's door.

She turned to me as I stood there looking back at her.

"No, I'll call them. I think it'll be good for me to talk to them. I don't mind, really." She patted my shoulder.

"Okay."

"You need to be with your husband right now. Call me later, okay."

"Okay, Jill. Call me if you need anything," I said, wrapping my arms around her in a big hug.

As we both pulled away, we wiped our eyes, and I headed into my house, waiting for Bryan to arrive.

"Your mom overdosed?"

"Yeah, she's been pretty upset. I guess my dad has been calling her. She was so scared, Bryan," I said, crying into my hands.

He sat next to me on the couch and pulled my head into his shoulder.

"Oh, Dez, I'm so sorry. I know the two of you had your problems, but this is your mom."

"Do you think he was really after her? I just wish I could remember what he did to her or what he looked like."

He raised my chin so his face was just inches from mine. "I will tell you what, tomorrow I will go into the station and make a few phone calls and find out where he is. If he had anything to do with this, I will find out."

"Thanks, Bryan. I'm so glad you are here."

"I'm not leaving. Why don't you go put on a comfy t-shirt and I will meet you upstairs, okay?"

"Well, I think I need a shower first. I think a nice hot shower would feel so good right now, then I'd love to meet you up there. Thanks, Bryan," I said as I began walking to the stairs.

"No problem, Dez. I'm here. I'm just going to make a phone call. Relax," he said grabbing his phone and flashing me a smile and those sexy dimples before walking away from me and into the kitchen.

He's probably calling Olivia.

I WALKED into my bedroom with my towel around me. He was lying on the bed, a magazine in his hands. He looked at me and I saw him blush as I grabbed my t-shirt and under-wear from the drawer. This made me feel better, but I still felt empty and sick inside from the loss of my mom.

"I have to use the bathroom anyway, you can get dressed in here."

As soon as I heard the bathroom door shut, I quickly changed and jumped under the covers before he got back. Was he really going to sleep in here with me tonight? I needed him so badly.

"Would you like me to stay the night with you?'

I turned toward him, wondering if he heard my thoughts somehow.

"I would like that. I just can't believe she's gone," I cried out, unable to hold back the tears. My eyes were swollen and itchy from all the crying, but somehow I just felt so much better wrapped in his arms as he held me tight throughout the night. I began feeling numb, which was so much better than sick to my stomach. He rubbed my head as I sat there praying that he wouldn't leave my side. I needed his forgiveness right now more than ever. I don't think I could go on without him.

He was always my strength when I needed him the most. My face rubbed against his soft, firm chest and my hands fingered his bulging biceps, calming me down. For just a second, I forgot about my mother's death and my failed marriage.

I closed my eyes, and that dreadful blonde popped into my head.

"Bryan, there is something I need to tell you."

"Shhh," he replied, rubbing my hair. Each stroke felt so relaxing as my eyes closed. "You can tell me tomorrow, just relax."

"Okay."

CHAPTER 20

The funeral was short and small. Since Mom didn't have a lot of friends, just close family and her two friends from work were there. Gabby was too young to really understand what was going on and didn't even cry during the funeral. Bryan was by my side, holding my hand as the pastor said a prayer for Mom. I no longer felt anything other than numb. Jill invited us over for a brunch after the burial.

"What did you make, Dez?" Jill asked, opening the tinfoil on the pan I was holding.

"Lasagna," I said, smiling.

"You know how much I love your lasagna. Gabby, you can go play pool downstairs if you want to. I set up the dollhouse too."

"Yay! Thanks Aunt Jill, you're the best," she said, jumping up and down before running off.

"So, where's Bryan?"

"He went to run home and change quick," I said, pouring myself a glass of Chardonnay.

"Ah. I noticed the two of you have sure been spending a lot of time together lately. Did you tell him?"

"No, I haven't told him yet. I have a feeling he will leave now that the funeral is over."

"Why haven't you told him yet?"

"I just don't think it will change anything. Plus, what if he confronts Olivia or Casey? What if he ruins things for him by getting custody of his son?"

"Really? What do you owe Casey, anyway?"

"It's not Casey, it's his son I am worried about. If she is that evil, I can't be the cause of a life of hell for him. My husband has a choice and if he wants to be with Olivia, there is nothing I can do or say to stop him," I said, sitting down to pout to myself.

"Snap out of it. Do you see the way he looks at you? I'm sorry, but if he didn't love you, he wouldn't be doing all of this for you. I think telling him will only add to the new relationship the two of you have already started."

"Oh, I don't know Jill."

She put her hand on my shoulder. "Trust me, I know. He is not into that girl or you would know by now. It's been, what, three days now? Four?"

"Five," I answered, taking a big gulp of my wine.

"Oh, he loves you. I wish I had a guy like yours. He rubs your feet, and he picks you up when you need him the most."

"Yeah, he's probably afraid I will become depressed again," I whined.

"Yeah, well, you don't look depressed to me, you look like you are grieving."

"I just can't believe she overdosed, Jill. We always said she wouldn't live a very long life the way she drank and did drugs, but I guess somewhere in the back of my mind I always thought she'd sober up before that."

"Mom would never sober up, you know that. We loved her and knew deep down she was an amazing mom. Only in a perfect world would she have ever returned to the mom we knew as kids."

"Did I miss anything?" Bryan asked, walking into the kitchen.

"No, just Jill bragging about how amazing my homemade lasagna is," I replied.

"Is there anything I can do to help?" he asked Jill.

"Yeah, kiss my sister and cheer her up," she replied, laughing.

"Oh, is that right?" he asked as he picked me up out of the chair and began lifting me over his shoulders like a sack of potatoes.

"No Bryan! Stop!" I screamed out, laughing and hitting his back.

"You asked for it," he joked, spinning in circles until I felt sick.

"Let me down, Bryan, please!" I screamed. "It's not funny, I feel sick."

He let me down, and it took me a minute for the room to stop spinning. He picked me up under my arms and I wrapped my legs around him, smiling. I didn't care that I felt like I would be sick from spinning, my mind was lost in the moment as I wrapped my arms around his head and pulled him in for a kiss.

As our lips touched, I felt happiness shoot through my entire body. I wasn't stressing about everything happening; I was only thinking about this amazing man coming back into my life again.

"Oh you two, get a room," Jill said, throwing a piece of garlic bread at us.

. . .

WE LAUGHED through dinner as we talked about memories we had as kids. We talked about how Jill let out the horses when she was four, so Mom would chase them when she was pregnant with me because she wanted to watch Mom's belly bounce.

We reminisced about when Gabby was a baby and Mom dyed her hair brown like mine because Gabby cried every time she held her. We were all laughing so hard we were crying. I didn't realize how much I loved my mom, even though I had to stay away when she was on her drinking binges. We were all going to miss her, but her wonderful memories would forever live on in us.

The night went on late into the evening, and we found Gabby fast asleep on the couch when we were finally ready to leave.

"Just let her stay," Jill said, winking at me.

"Are you sure?" I asked.

"I'm sure, now go home and tell your husband you didn't screw his best friend," she whispered in my ear.

I nodded back, "Thanks Jill, I owe you."

"You sure do."

WE WERE both silent on the drive home as I thought about whether I should tell him the truth. As we pulled up to the house, I saw someone sitting on our steps. We got out of the car as Casey stood up.

"What the hell are you doing here? Leave now! I know what you did to Dez. Get out!" Bryan screamed.

"I need to talk to you, just listen, please!"

I looked at Bryan and touched his arm. He was about to yell something until he felt my touch and he turned to me with a confused look on his face.

"Listen to him, please."

He raised his eyebrows and looked from me to Casey, and then we followed him as he unlocked the door and headed into the dining room. We all sat down at the table, Bryan still looked like he was in shock from my words.

"Destiny and I did not sleep together."

"What? Please don't even bring that up, we've moved past that," Bryan said back, getting up from his chair.

I stood up too and guided him back down to his chair. "Please, just let him continue."

He looked shocked, mortified, even angrier at my words.

"I don't understand," he said to me.

"In high school, Olivia showed up at my house. It was the night she tried to get you to have sex with her in the hot tub, remember?"

"What does Olivia have to do with anything? And why are you bringing up high school?" he screamed at him.

"Listen!" he screamed back. "Olivia showed up at my house upset, one thing led to another and I had sex with her."

"You screwed not only my wife, but my girlfriend too, and you found the need to rub it in my face after all these years!" Bryan shouted again, as a vein in his forehead popped out in response. He stood up again.

"Please sit down!" I scolded him. "Listen."

He took a deep breath and glared at me.

"Bryan, she left after high school because she was pregnant with my child. She didn't want you to know," Casey admitted, looking down with shame.

"You knocked her up? What did she do with the baby? I can't believe you! How could you?"

"There's more."

"How much more can there be?" Bryan said, now standing. I didn't even try to get him to sit down again. I was sure he just about had it with me too.

"Calm down. I didn't know for nine years. When my dad

was dying, she called me out of the blue and told me we had a child. She told me I would only get to see him if I broke the two of you up. Bryan I'm sorry."

"What did you do?" His expression softened a bit when he looked at me again.

"Olivia gave me a Roofie to slip into Dez's drink."

"You raped her!" he screamed, running around the table and tackling him.

"Stop it, Bryan! Stop it! He didn't rape me!" I yelled, trying to pull him off Casey. He needed to finish.

His elbow came back and hit me right in the face. My nose began bleeding profusely as Bryan quickly stopped and ran to get me a towel.

"I'm so sorry Dez, why did you try to pull me off him? Aren't you mad what he did to you?"

"Bryan, I knew, he told me," I admitted, holding my nostrils closed with the towel.

He began backing away from me, "Why didn't you tell me?"

"Please, let Casey finish," I pleaded.

He turned and looked at Casey.

"I didn't tell you at the time because Olivia told me if I didn't break the two of you up she would never let me see my son. You don't understand, she is mean to him, hits him. He hates her and wants to live with me. I told Dez I needed Liv to sign the paperwork before she could tell you, for my son's safety."

"You don't owe him anything!" Bryan screamed to me with such anger, I felt like I didn't even know him.

"It's his son, Bryan. I couldn't do that to his son," I began crying.

My eyes were swollen, and my nose was bleeding. I didn't expect the night to end like this.

"Did she sign the papers?" Bryan asked.

"No, she won't answer my calls and she knows you've been with Destiny."

"I just can't believe she's been playing me all this time," Bryan said, turning to me. "I'm so sorry I didn't believe you when you told me you didn't remember sleeping with him. I'm so sorry."

"It's okay, you didn't know," I said, putting my hand on the side of his face.

"I'm sorry, Bryan," Casey said, walking up behind him.

Bryan turned around fast, putting his hands around Casey's neck.

"Get the hell out! Get the hell out and never come back!" he shouted, pushing him out the door and slamming it in his face. He locked the door and came back to me on the chair and kissed my forehead.

"I'm so sorry baby, I love you so much. I am such a jerk, such a jerk."

"I love you, Bryan."

I pulled the towel away from my face, realizing it wasn't bleeding anymore, and threw it on the ground. I ran up to Bryan and wrapped my arms around him and squeezed as tight as I could.

"Nothing will ever get between us again, Dez. I promise."

"Are you going to talk to Casey again?" I asked, worried.

"I'll figure this all out tomorrow. I just couldn't listen to him anymore."

"I understand," I said, resting my head on his chest.

CHAPTER 21

$\mathcal{I}$ woke up with my head on his chest and a smile on my face. I lifted my head and strained my neck to see if his eyes were open. I must have woken him up with my movement, because his eyes blinked open and he rubbed them with his free arm.

"Well, I must say you continue to surprise me, Dez."

I moved away so I could see him easier and rested my head on my hand with my elbow as the base. I didn't want him to get a whiff of my morning breath, so I talked without opening my mouth too wide.

"Why do you say that?" I asked, smiling.

"Cause you are just amazing," he replied, looking up at me.

I rested my chin on his chest and stared into his eyes as he raised his head by folding the pillow underneath him as he talked.

"I'm not amazing. I almost lost you."

"Are you kidding me? I didn't trust you. I thought you slept with my best friend. This is more my fault than yours. My crazy ex-girlfriend from high school has been setting up our marriage for failure and I didn't even notice. How did I not not catch this?"

"I don't know. What matters now is that we move on together," I said, sitting up.

"I need to make this right."

"How? What do you mean? What are you going to do?"

"I have a plan, I will make this right, okay? Just trust me," he said, sitting up and kissing me.

His kiss lasted longer than planned as I pulled his head in every time he tried to pull away. The kiss became harder as he pushed me onto my back and ran his hands down my body.

"We can finish this tonight, I need to fix this," he said, getting up and putting his shirt on.

"What's your plan? I want to know."

I struggled to keep my swollen, dry eyes open. As I rubbed my eyes, I began thinking about my mom again. I should have helped her while she was alive. Why didn't I try harder?

"Just trust me, okay. I will be back by dinnertime."

I nodded at him as he kissed me on the forehead and grabbed his keys off the nightstand. I rolled onto his side of the bed and smelled his pillow as I hugged it in my arms. I was too tired to think about what he was up to. I trusted him, and that is all that matters. Now I just need to focus on getting up and getting ready so I can pick up Gabby from Jill's.

By DINNERTIME, Bryan still wasn't home yet, and I got worried. I cooked dinner for Gabby; she took a bath, and I just started reading to her when I heard the front door open. As I read *The Velveteen Rabbit*, I couldn't think about one word I was reading aloud. I wanted to rush downstairs and find out what he was doing all day. I didn't even realize Gabby was sleeping as I finished up the last page and put the book down and pulled up her blanket to tuck her in.

"I love you Gabby," I whispered, tiptoeing out of her room and quietly shutting the door.

I headed down the stairs to find Bryan sitting on the couch with papers in his hand.

"Hey you, I was getting worried. How did it go today? I want to hear everything," I said, plopping down on the couch next to him.

He turned toward me with red eyes, wiping a tear that was stuck in the corner of his eye. Why did I feel so nervous suddenly? He looked so sad.

"Well, when I left here, I went to Casey's house. He gave me the paperwork Liv needed to sign so he could get custody of his son."

"Did he draft up the paperwork himself?"

"No, his partner did."

"Oh," I responded, flashing him a warm smile to show him I was here for him. I grabbed his hand as he continued.

"Casey and I drove to Duluth. Liv was home."

"Was she surprised to see the two of you together?"

"Oh yeah. The look in her eyes explained it all. Luckily, Travis was at the neighbor's house when we got there, so he didn't have to hear what was going on. She apologized up and down and quickly signed over custody to Casey. Then she asked to talk to me alone."

My eyes got big, and I pulled my hand away from him, turning away so he couldn't see the jealousy and fear in my expression.

"It's okay, Destiny, look at me."

I turned my head toward him, and he wiped my tears.

"She tried to kiss me, but I pushed her away. I don't love her, Dez, I love you. You know that. may have told you I wasn't in love with you anymore, but I was fighting the powerful feelings I have for you. You mean the world to me and always have. From the moment I first laid eyes on you in college, I knew you were the one. There was something about you. I just can't explain it. I gravitated to you, could never get enough. You have my heart always and forever," he said, grabbing my chin and pulling my face in to his.

We rubbed noses as our lips touched just lightly. His big soft lips pressed against mine and neither one of us closed our eyes. We didn't want to miss a moment by blinking. My heart no longer heavy with guilt and shame. I would never take this relationship for granted ever again.

"I love you," I whispered softly.

"I love you too. It's over, Destiny, it's over," he whispered back.

"How do you know she will not bother us anymore?"

"I don't know that, but I won't let that happen again. She promised me she would never contact me again. She also promised to get help. Destiny, she admitted, she's bipolar. She's been off her meds. She's sick, she just needs help. Casey even agreed to let her take Travis whenever she wanted after she got the help she needs."

"Wow, I can't believe he is the same person I was so scared of not so long ago," I said, leaning back on the couch.

"I know. Enough about Casey. How are you doing? I know this can't be easy for you, after just losing your mom and then dealing with all of this."

"You're right, it's not easy, but I'm doing okay. I screamed in my car on the way to pick up Gabby this morning. I screamed at my mom, told her I hated her," I confessed, laughing at myself.

"That's normal, Destiny. You are angry at her for being so reckless, for all those years she hurt you and your sister. You know there was nothing you could do to help her. She didn't believe she had a problem."

He put his arm around me, squeezing me into him.

"I know, I just wish I could have helped her."

"It's going to take time. I am here. I won't leave your side. I mean, other than work," he teased.

"I want to find another job. I want to work again. Gabby is in school now, I don't need to stay home anymore."

"I think that's a great idea, if that's what you want. I support you no matter what you want to do."

I jumped on his lap, put my arms around his neck and felt my heart exploding with every second our lips met. He pushed my arms up in the air and pulled my shirt over my head.

"What about Gabby," I whispered, giggling.

"Isn't she sleeping?"

"Well, yeah."

"Then what about Gabby?" he asked, pushing me onto my back.

His lips were soft as he made his way down to my navel, soft and wet kisses enveloped my body, leaving me gasping for air.

We took it slow, enjoying every inch of each other's bodies. His hands ran down my back, massaging its way down to my ankles. His touch was soft, light, and left me desiring more. I squeezed every muscle in his body with my hands, appreciating every push-up and pull-up that made them this firm. His body was soft, I desired more of him, now. I stopped and stared into his blue eyes, watching his dimples appear in the shadows of the light. This is the man I want to spend the rest of my life with. I felt like that young girl in college, running toward him with plans of bumping into him, just to touch him. I never thought we would get to this point. Now I'm his wife, holding his big, firm body in my hands, squeezing him.

As we made love, all I could think about was our happy ending. I thanked God for sending him back to me. I decided then and there, I was the only one who could decide my happiness. It was my choice to seize the day or engulf my mind in negative thoughts, feeling sorry for myself. It was time to finally choose me.

CHAPTER 22

We spent the next couple of months training for Grandma's marathon, the largest marathon in Minnesota. People came from all over just to run the race, due to the beautiful coastal view of Lake Superior along with the majority of the race. So many spectators cheered the runners on. It was well-known for being one of the funnest marathons. Around nine thousand people ran the full marathon. They named it after Grandma's Restaurant because it was the only business in Duluth that would sponsor the race. As a child, my dream was to run Grandma's Marathon.

We wanted to run our first full-marathon together. I found a job working for a local insurance company, making significant money and finally feeling the happiness I long desired.

ON JUNE twenty-second of nineteen ninety-seven, we drove to Duluth at four o'clock in the morning. We took a bus to the starting line on the North Shore, where it was cold, dark, and stinky from the port-a-john's that lined both sides of the street. We watched the sun come up as we stretched each other out in the grass.

As the announcer instructed everyone to get to the starting line, I felt sick at the thought of running twenty-six point two miles.

"Do you know how a marathon became a marathon?" I asked him, stretching my arms behind my back.

"No, Mrs. Fredrickson, how?" he asked, laughing at my nerves.

"The legend has it that a Greek messenger named Pheidippides ran from the city of Marathon all the way to Athens to deliver a message that the Greeks won against the Persians in the Battle of Marathon."

"Oh, really?"

"Just let me finish," I snapped, playfully. "The man made it the twenty-six point two miles and delivered his message, then fell over and died, died."

"Well, legend has it they aren't even sure exactly how far it was. They estimated it to be around twenty-six miles, and this happened in four hundred-ninety BC. That was before they had Gatorade," he said, laughing. "And, you forget, we have been training a long time for this, including a twenty-mile run just two weeks ago. Don't tell me you forgot about that, because I don't think I will ever forget it."

"I'm just saying, he died. We've never run that far," I said, feeling my face growing hot as the countdown began.

"Let's just take it one mile at a time, okay? I will be by your side the whole way."

He kissed me, but I was too nervous to enjoy it.

"Just remember, Gabby and Jill will wait for us at the finish."

I smiled and thought of her sweet face and how proud she will be when she sees us complete a marathon.

As the gun went off, we tried not to think about how many miles we had to go, and instead focused on appreciating every mile we made it. By mile twenty, I was sure my legs would fall off, but Bryan ran backwards, cheering me on. I rolled my eyes in response; I was dying.

As we neared Canal Park, I could hear the music and cheering. I pushed harder than I have ever had to push. I thought about the man that fell over and died, and I knew it had to be accurate. There was no way I could stop running and walk, for I feared the pain would set in and I wouldn't be able to take another step. My legs felt so heavy, I mentally had to picture myself picking them up one at a time with each step. Almost there. My arms were chafing as I passed a man with two bloody circles on his white shirt where his nipples would be. I felt so horrible for him. I looked at Bryan to make sure his weren't bleeding and was glad to see his gray shirt was just wet with sweat.

We hit the twenty-six mile mark, and I broke down.

"I can't, I just can't go any further," I cried out to him.

"You can do this, Dez. You have made it twenty-six miles and you only have point two of a mile left. Give it everything you've got, do it for Gabby."

As soon as he said her name, I dug some energy from somewhere so deep within. My desire to finish and hug her numbed the pain. I pushed and pushed, focusing on swinging my arms faster, harder. Bryan stayed beside me. As we crossed the finish line together, he grabbed my arm and raised it in the air as we smiled at each other and slowed down. Tears streaked down my face at the feeling of accomplishment. The pain we endured, the hours of training. I was so proud of myself for pulling it together and finishing.

The medal they placed over my head was heavy, and I wasn't sure I could support the weight. I grabbed a bottle of water off the table in front of me as I scanned the crowd for my baby girl. Bryan kissed me, but I pulled away quickly, unable to breathe. I began falling over. He held me up.

"You can't sit yet, you will cramp up. You just need to walk. Let's find Gabby."

I focused on putting one foot in front of the other, but I was dizzy, everything hurt. I could not feel my feet, yet I could feel all the blisters that stabbed me with each step I took. My toes hurt, and I wondered if I had any nails left at all. A picture of them black and falling off seemed accurate right about now.

I looked up and saw her smiling face as she came running right into my arms. I didn't care about the pain and I didn't even notice I was falling over as I leaned in for a hug. Bryan caught me, saving us both from falling to the ground. We all erupted in laughs.

"I can't believe you ran that far, Mom!" she shouted in excitement.

"Congrats, girl. I don't think I could ever finish a marathon. You didn't let the miles beat you, good job," Jill said hugging me. "Although you are very sweaty, yuck."

I laughed, still unable to talk as my body just felt utterly exhausted.

"Can we go home now?" I asked Bryan.

"What, you don't want to stay for the band?" he said, laughing.

"If I had the energy, I think I would punch you right now for not being in as much pain as I am. Why did we sign up for this again?" I asked him sarcastically.

WE SPENT the next day in ice baths, extreme cramping in both of our legs. Although I could hardly walk from the blisters on my feet, it was definitely worth the feeling of accomplishment after running for five and a half hours.

We headed out to our cabin, twenty minutes north of town, the following day. Casey and Travis met us out there for boating and waterskiing. Although we knew we'd never be as close to Casey again, we were still friends. I could never forget what he put me through, but I found it in my heart with some convincing from Bryan to forgive him for what he did. I knew deep in his heart he thought he was doing the right thing. Olivia was controlling him, and it was much easier for me to blame her.

Although Bryan forgave Olivia for what she did, I just couldn't find it in my heart to forgive her. Bryan told me once I did, it would free my soul, whatever that means. I felt just fine hating her. It's not like I'd ever have to see her again, or so I thought.

CHAPTER 23

AUGUST 1997

"So, I was thinking about the three of us driving down to the Cities this weekend, maybe doing some school clothes shopping and going to Camp Snoopy," Bryan said, acting all giddy.

"Hmm, I think that sounds like a great idea. You don't mind shopping with two girls all day?"

"I don't mind at all," he said, kissing me.

I grabbed him tighter, enjoying every second of feeling like a new bride in his arms.

"You don't mind if I skip the rides this time?" I asked, trying to hide my smile.

"But you love the rides. Why don't you want to go on any rides?"

I cleared my throat and tried to look as serious as I could manage. "Because they won't let pregnant women on the rides."

His eyes got huge as he picked me up in the air. I wrapped my legs around him as our kiss was deep and hard, his teeth knocking against mine in excitement. Although it hurt, I didn't even let out a word because I couldn't ruin the moment.

"We are having a baby!" he screamed. "Does Gabby know?"

I shook my head.

"Can we tell her? Can we? She will be so excited. How long have you known?"

"I knew I was late, but I didn't know for sure until I took the pregnancy test just a minute ago."

He hugged me again, squeezing me a little too hard. "Let's go tell Gabby she will be a big sister!" he yelled in excitement, grabbing my hand and pulling me down the hallway. I had to practically run just to keep up with him.

He knocked on her door.

"Gabby," he said, walking in.

She put down her Barbies and stood up.

"Everything okay? Why do you guys look so weird right now?" she asked, pushing her eyebrows together in curiosity.

"How would you feel about being a big sister?"

"Seriously? Are you really having a baby?" she screamed, jumping up and down.

"Yes, you will be a big sister," I announced, picking her up in my arms. Bryan joined in on the family hug and we all fell onto her bed, laughing with excitement and tickling each other.

"Is it a boy or a girl?" she asked once we all stopped laughing and stood back up.

"It's too early to tell. You will be the first to know," I told her, kissing the top of her head.

"How would you like to celebrate by going to the Cities

and going shopping at The Mall of America and maybe going on some rides?"

His question was followed by some loud screaming, which left us both covering our ears.

Bryan turned to me. "I guess that's a yes."

She jumped up and down, making her way to her bed to jump up and down.

"No jumping on the bed," I announced, firmly.

"Well, I'm going to work. You two best get packing, we are going to Minneapolis in just two days."

With that, the screaming continued and Bryan and I closed the door and escaped quickly.

"Thanks for getting her all riled up before you go to work," I teased, crossing my arms around his neck.

His kiss was passionate, and I felt butterflies again. I didn't want him to leave.

"We will finish this after I get home tonight." He smiled, slapping my butt.

I ran behind him and jumped on his back. He caught me and began spinning me around and then dropping me on the couch. He pinned my hands behind my head and came down just inches from my face.

"I love you, Destiny. Always have and always will. I can't wait to have another baby or four," he said, kissing me before heading out the door.

"Let's start with one, okay. Be safe!" I yelled after him.

I didn't notice that he left his bulletproof vest on the counter in the kitchen.

JILL AND I met at Mom's house to finish going through her things before we sold her house. She left it in her will for us, but neither one of us wanted to live there, be reminded of what happened there.

"So, where's Gabby today?" Jill asked, throwing another sweater into the garage sale bin.

"She's at Bryan's parents' house. I figured this would be too much for her."

"Oh yeah, I agree.

"Did you hear that?" I asked, wondering what the loud noise was downstairs.

"Yes," she said, getting up and making her way toward the noise. I grabbed the bin and headed down after her.

We walked into the kitchen and there he stood. I didn't have any pictures of him, but he looked just like Jill. I knew it was him immediately.

"Where's Kim!" he screamed, pointing a gun at us.

I dropped the bin on the floor and we both put our hands up in the air.

"She passed away a few months ago," Jill responded. "Dad, it's me, Jill. Please put the gun away."

I could tell he was drunk, possibly high. His pupils were dilated, his eyes red, and the smell of whisky filled the room.

"Jill?" he asked, slightly putting the gun down. It had been aimed right at her face.

"Yes, dad, it's me."

"Where is she? I know she isn't dead," he said, his words slurred, gun raising back up.

"Dad, put the gun down and I will talk to you," Jill said, as calmly as she could.

He pointed the gun down again.

"Destiny, why don't you go get Dad another shirt, it looks like his is all wet."

I nodded at her, understanding her hint. They stood there talking as I ran upstairs and dialed nine-one-one. I sat on the phone with the operator, telling her everything that happened and what I knew. Although the operator advised me against it, I hung up the phone and ran downstairs with a shirt for Andrew. I didn't want her to be alone with him. My hands were shaky and Jill's voice began to shake too as she tried talking Dad down and keeping his mind occupied until the cops arrived.

Within minutes, Bryan poked his head around the corner of the kitchen.

Dad stood up quickly, raising his gun.

"Mr. Lawson, please put the gun down," my husband ordered him in a voice I didn't even recognize.

Bryan's gun was drawn, as was Andrew's.

"How do you know my name?"

"I'm Destiny's husband. Now let's put the guns down and have a talk," Bryan said calmly, starting to lower his gun as he held his other hand up in the air.

"Bryan, don't," I yelled out, crying in fear.

"You called the police?" Andrew shouted, now pointing the gun at me.

My ears felt hollow as I heard the many shots fired. It all happened so fast, yet in slow motion. As I came to, I realized I was on the ground and someone heavy was on top of me, crushing me. I heard the blood-curdling screams and realized it was mine. My body was bloody, I couldn't get up. That's when I looked up and saw the horror in Jill's face as she pulled the man in uniform off me. Policemen and paramedics filled the room, and I could no longer breathe.

CHAPTER 24

I woke up in a hospital, an IV in my arm. Jill by my
side, still crying.

"What happened?" I asked. "Was I shot?"

Jill came closer and held my hand.

"No, Dez, you will be okay," she said, except she seemed
to look even sadder as she talked.

"What is it, Jill?" I asked, feeling the shooting pain in my
ribs. "Who was on top of me? Was that our dad? Was he
shot?"

"Dad was shot and killed, honey," She said, putting my
hair behind my ears.

I could see the sadness in her eyes, there was more she
wasn't telling me.

"What is it, Jill? Tell me," I said, anger and frustration
breaking through my voice.

"Dad's dead, but it's Bryan," she cried out, sobbing hyster-
ically into her hands. "I'm so sorry, I'm so sorry."

"What happened, Jill! What happened to Bryan?" I yelled,
even more frustrated with her stupid brief hints.

"He shot Dad and Dad shot him too. Destiny, I'm so sorry.

141

They are both dead. He was gone when the paramedics arrived. He shot him right in the chest," she said, holding my hands.

I pushed her hands away.

"No, he didn't! You're lying, you're lying! Tell me the truth, tell me where he is, Jill! I want him, I need him. Tell me you're lying, just tell me!" I screamed, sitting up and ignoring the excruciating pain that took my breath away as I sat up.

"I'm so sorry," she replied, standing up and backing away from me.

I grabbed everything off the tray next to me and began throwing it at the door. I could hear Jill crying louder on the other side of the room.

"Get out! Just get out!" I screamed at her.

"I'm so sorry, Dez, I'm so sorry," she repeated, running out the door and looking back with even more sadness.

I pushed the call button for the nurses as I caught my breath and calmed down slightly. The blonde ran in the door just a minute later.

"Where is my husband?" I said, not wanting to believe what Jill told me. She had to be lying, unsure of the truth.

Two more nurses came in the door, along with a security guard from the hospital.

She looked at me like I was a sad, broken child.

"I'm so sorry, Mrs. Fredrickson, he passed away."

I held my breath and fought the anxiety that was weakening every muscle in my body. My heart felt broken as the anger turned to pain and sadness. I cried out for him, hugging my legs to my chest. I held my breath and squeezed my chest hard, wanting to be taken from this world to be with him. What was my life without him in it?

"Careful Mrs., you have a broken rib," she warned me, running to my side.

She grabbed a tissue from the box next to the bed and handed it to me so I could blow my nose and wipe my eyes.

"I'm so sorry. Is there anything I can do?"

"Is my baby okay?" I asked, feeling like someone was jumping on my heart and sucking all the blood out.

"Your baby boy will be fine. You just need plenty of rest. Would you like me to get your sister for you now?" she said, extreme empathy showing through her voice and a frown on her face.

"Yes, please," I answered, as the rest of the crew left the room.

She looked back at me before going to get Jill.

"Your husband is a hero, Mrs. Fredrickson. He jumped in front of the bullet when that man tried to kill you."

I felt the blood empty from my face. He saved my life and my dad tried to end it.

WHEN JILL RETURNED, I apologized, and she crawled into the bed with me, holding me tight. I winced in pain a few times, but all I could think about was having to tell Gabby and live the rest of my life without him by my side. I cried and cried, screaming out in excruciating pain from the burning in my heart.

"How do I go on, Jill, without Bryan? He was everything."

She picked up her head and ran her hand across my cheek.

"You do it for Gabby and your baby boy. You can't give up, not without a fight. Bryan wouldn't want you to be unhappy."

"I can't do this alone," I cried. "How do you know it's a boy?"

"The nurse told me. You won't be alone. I am right here by your side. I can move in and help you raise the kids."

"I can't let you stop living your life for me."

"I want to. For you, for the kids. I am here as long as you need me."

And she did. She was there when I told Gabby about the passing of her father, the hero. She was there by my side at his funeral and she was there those mornings I couldn't pull myself out of bed. She was there to talk me into seeing a therapist, and she was there to open the shades and make me get on with my day when the depression set in. She was there when my baby boy, Matthew Bryan Fredrickson, was born, holding my hand and taking turns changing his poopy diapers.

She was there when I ran my next marathon, with my children by her side at the finish line as I completed it. She fell in love with a guy she met at work, and I finally convinced her to leave and marry him once he proposed. She was still there as much as she could be.

The day her daughter, Elizabeth Destiny, was born, I couldn't be prouder of her success. She had everything she wanted in life and more. As my children grew up, I never moved on. The only man I wanted in my life was Bryan, and I knew one day we would meet again. I was content with my kids, running, and work. I became an editor for the Duluth News Tribune and moved after Gabby graduated from high school. She attended The University of Duluth, majoring in Social Work. The day Matthew graduated from Denfield High School, I saw a beautiful blonde in the crowd.

I came up behind her and tapped her on the shoulder.

"Hello, Olivia."

She looked surprised to see me, scared of what I would say next.

"I'm so sorry to hear about Bryan," she said with teary eyes.

"That was years ago, but thank you. I just wanted to tell you I forgive you."

She looked at me, happiness in her eyes as a smile spread across her perfect face.

"You have no idea how much that means to me. Do you have a child graduating today?"

"Yes, our son Matthew. How about you? Married, more kids?"

"My stepson," she said, pointing to her ring. "I am married now, to a doctor from St. Mary's. He's an oncologist, a great man."

"I'm so happy for you," I said, looking over her shoulder to see Matthew searching for me in the crowd.

"I have to go, but it was so great seeing you."

Bryan was right, it felt so good to forgive. I smiled as I wrapped my baby in my arms, thankful to have raised such a sweet boy who was now a man.

I smiled, thinking of the day my husband graduated from Bemidji State. The uproar of cheers as they handed him his diploma.

"I can't believe I did it, Mom," he said, hugging me.

"Oh, I can believe it. You remind me so much of your dad."

"I wish I could have met him," he said, sadly.

"Oh Matt, he's right here with us. He's always right here," I said, pointing to his heart, and he smiled.

CHAPTER 25

JANUARY 2017

I opened my eyes and saw his father's eyes looking back at me. He truly had his eyes, his dimples, his nose. I looked around the room and saw Bryan standing behind Gabby, waiting for me in his flannel shirt. He was smiling, his dimples defined. He was still young and handsome as he stared at me. He put his hands on Matthew's shoulders, and that's when I realized they were wearing the same shirt. I wondered if Matthew could see him or feel his presence.

I closed my eyes to rest them for a moment and drifted off to sleep.

"What is that horrible noise coming from her? Can't she breathe?" I heard Gabby ask.

"That is called the death rattle. It sounds almost like a gurgling or choking sound. Although it is horrible for us to hear, it really doesn't bother her. I can try to sit her up a little so it's not so loud. I know it sounds horrifying."

"Yes, please."

I could hear Matthew's sobs. I wanted to comfort him, hold him in my arms one last time.

"We need to let her go, Gabby. We need to tell her it's okay."

"I'm not ready, I'm not ready," she cried out, squeezing my hand.

"Look at her, she will not get better. She has been through enough. We need to do this for her."

I could no longer open my eyes or move at all. One minute I could hear them talking, and the next minute I was running through fields holding Bryan's hand again.

I wasn't sure what was real and what wasn't anymore.

"It's not about you anymore. She needs to be at peace, be with dad again."

"Oh, Mom!"

"You heard the hospice nurse, she can go any time now. We need to say our goodbyes," he whispered to her.

"I can't," she said back.

"Gabby, you need to let her go. Do you really want her to live like this? Just let her go."

I could feel the love in the room, could feel the aura of sadness and pain that surrounded my bed. I now realized I was having a hard time telling Matthew and my husband apart. When was Matthew in the room? When was my husband really there? I felt confused, unsure of what was real and what wasn't. How could I have forgotten my husband was already dead?

She took a deep breath, "Mom, I love you so much. I don't want you to leave me, I'm not ready yet. But I will never be ready. You have been there for me through the most troublesome times in my life and even when I was a horrible teenager," she let out a laugh through her tears.

"It's okay," I heard Matthew assure her.

"You are my best friend. I can't imagine this world without you. I know it's time for you to be with Daddy in heaven. He has been waiting so long for you. We will never forget you. Your love will forever live on in my heart. I can only wish to be half the mother you have been for me..." her voice cut off as she ran out of breath, unable to talk anymore.

"Mom, what can I say, you have been there for me through everything in my life. The thought of my children not being able to make cakes with you or have sleepovers and play chess just breaks my heart. I know that you fought as hard as you could, but you have suffered long enough. We will be okay. I love you so much and I am so sorry you had to suffer like this."

I felt him kiss my cheek.

"I love you, Mom. It's time for you to leave us now and go see Dad and Grandma in heaven. We will be okay, I promise. It's time," she said, kissing my forehead and squeezing my hand.

"You are the best sister a girl could ever ask for. I will take care of your grandchildren like my own and tell them all about our crazy adventures. I got this from here. Go to that husband of yours. He's been waiting patiently for you for far too long. You will always be my best friend. I love you so much," Jill said, just inches from my face.

THAT NIGHT, I took Bryan's hand and watched myself leave my home and the bed I was in for so long. I turned back and saw Jill sleeping on the couch, sitting up, with Gabby's head on her shoulder. Matthew fell asleep on the floor next to my bed, afraid to leave my side.

I blew them a kiss and smiled as I squeezed Bryan's hand and watched my body turn back into it's thirty-year-old self. I felt strong and happy and free.

"It's about time," Bryan said, picking me up and spinning me around. "You have no idea how much I've missed you."

"I've missed you so much," I said, kissing him. I never had to have another moment without him ever again.

"They will be okay, I promise. We won't miss a thing," he said, taking my hand again.

"I know," I said, walking side by side with him into the light. "I know."

ACKNOWLEDGMENTS

With special thanks to my husband, Owen Walters. Without you, I wouldn't be who I am today. You have been there with me through the hardest days of my life and have always pushed me to be the best me I can be. Thank you so much for everything you do to support me, always. You are not only my best friend, but my partner. Thanks for taking hours to read this with me out loud to help me perfect it.

Thank you to my girls, Sidney and Alexis. I am so proud of both of you. Never give up on your dreams. You are my whole world and I love you both very much.

Thanks to my accountability buddy, Reiley Wieland, you helped to keep me on track and were always there for me when I needed you. I am so honored to have met you and I know our friendship will last forever.

Big thanks to The Deception of Destiny launch team! You helped me shape this book into what it has become. Thank you so much for all your hard work. I couldn't have done it without you!

With special thanks to the best editor I could ever ask for, Allison Goddard. You are amazing!

And last, but not least, the SPS community. You are truly like family; the immense support is unbelievable and invaluable.